A Bridge
Between Us

ANCHOR BOOKS
DOUBLEDAY
New York   London   Toronto   Sydney   Auckland

A Bridge Between Us

Julie Shigekuni

AN ANCHOR BOOK
PUBLISHED BY DOUBLEDAY
a division of Bantam Doubleday Dell Publishing Group, Inc.
1540 Broadway, New York, New York 10036

ANCHOR BOOKS, DOUBLEDAY, and the portrayal of an anchor
are trademarks of Doubleday, a division of
Bantam Doubleday Dell Publishing Group. Inc.

Book Design by Gretchen Achilles
Interior Illustrations © 1995 by Jonathan Glick.

"Metaphors" is from Crossing the Water by Sylvia Plath.
Copyright © 1960 by Ted Hughes. Copyright renewed.
Reprinted by permission of HarperCollins Publishers, Inc.

Library of Congress Cataloging-in-Publication Data

Shigekuni, Julie.
A bridge between us / Julie Shigekuni. — 1st ed.
p. cm.
1. Japanese American families—California, Northern—Fiction.
2. Japanese American women—California, Northern—Fiction.
3. Family—California, Northern—Fiction. I. Title.
PS3569.H4865B75 1995

813'.54—dc20
94-3668
CIP

ISBN 0-385-47678-7

10 9 8 7 6 5 4 3 2 1

FIRST EDITION

"If you move from what is to what may be,
you pass over a bridge which takes you from
Hell to Paradise. And the strangest thing:
a Paradise made of precisely the same material
of which Hell is made. It is only the perception
of the order of the materials that differs . . ."

ODYSSEAS ELYTIS
from Open Book

In memory of my grandmothers,
LILLIAN YURIKO SHIGEKUNI and
MASUKO KIKUMURA,
and for Jonathan

Acknowledgments

For generous support during the writing of this book, I thank The Henfield Foundation, The Millay Colony for the Arts, The MacDowell Colony, Inc., Cummington Community for the Arts, and The American Japanese National Literary Award. And for their careful reading of this book in its various stages: Jerome Badanes, E. M. Broner, Albert Reed, Deneen Jenks, Brooke Mitchell, Eileen Penner, Ann Patchett, and Marion Shigekuni.

This book would not have been possible without the patience and encouragement of Linsey Abrams, Virginia Nicholson, and Spencer Newman.

And for assistance with research, I am indebted to Laurie Shigekuni Gong, Stanton Gong, Phil Shigekuni, and Akemi Kikumura.

Contents

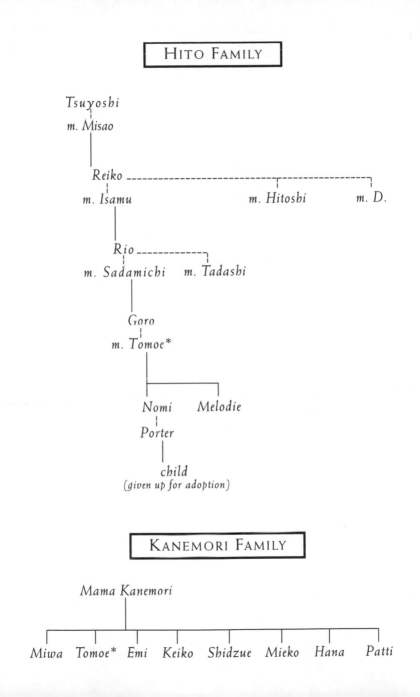

HITO FAMILY

Tsuyoshi
m. Misao

Reiko
m. Isamu   m. Hitoshi   m. D.

Rio
m. Sadamichi   m. Tadashi

Goro
m. Tomoe*

Nomi   Melodie
Porter

child
(given up for adoption)

KANEMORI FAMILY

Mama Kanemori

Miwa   Tomoe*   Emi   Keiko   Shidzue   Mieko   Hana   Patti

Lamp of Darkness

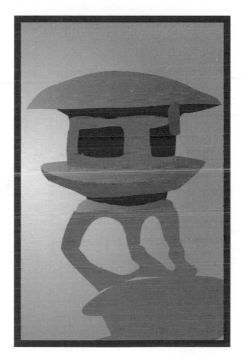

Prologue

·

Reiko

"Reiko, never forget who you are," my father told me. "You are the daughter of a princess." He held my hand in his as he spoke these words. I watched his pupils contract to points the size of distant stars, his flesh turn pale as an autumn moon. My father's fist turned to stone around my fingers, his spirit fled, and his body was left behind for me to dispose of.

The first thing I did was to lay my father's body across our kitchen table. Though this might have seemed a strange way to display a corpse, I did not act without thought. Since he arrived in San Francisco, my father's life had not been easy. Without the assistance of a wife, he had had neither the time nor the inclination to collect material possessions. The house was nothing like it is now —back then, it still belonged to my father. I remember the kitchen table was the only surface large and sturdy

enough to hold his weight, and I chose to leave the table
where it was, in the kitchen, because that is the room with
a view of San Francisco Bay where my father arrived from
Tokyo with my mother back in 1898. My father was a
sentimentalist, and I knew he would have appreciated such
a consideration. Despite his moderate years, he had fallen
ill, and for over a month his body had become too tender
to be properly bathed. But he had always been concerned,
for the sake of appearances, about hygiene. That night I
scrubbed him clean. I used scissors to remove his robe and
bedclothes, and then after giving his hair a thorough
washing, I trimmed and shaped it. I scoured his body beginning with the dark recesses of his nostrils and ears and
did not stop until his nails had been filed and properly
manicured. I even scrubbed the spaces between his fingers
and toes. By morning, when my first husband Isamu and
my daughter Rio awoke, my father was wearing his finest
silk kimono. His skin shone like ivory and his ceremonial
sword lay like a pillow beneath his head.

It was inconvenient for my family not to be able to eat
our meals in the kitchen, but I kept my father's body for a
full week. During that time I arranged for the funeral,
which was to be held in lavish style. In the large urn
beside the fireplace I still cherish what is left. Hair, toe
and nail clippings, the gold platings of teeth, and ashes are
all that remain to remind me who I am.

I have tried to live faithful to what I imagine it means

to live with the dignity and grace befitting my mother. And while my father told me I must not forget, it has not been easy now that my grandson's wife shouts *wake up* in my ear each morning like it is the eleventh commandment and lifts the black cloth mask from my eyes and throws the window open to let in the light and the noise from Mason Street below, as if I am an old woman who must be reminded it's not 1919 anymore. It is true. I fear I may not live much longer, yet I must not forget my father's words.

My father told me stories about my mother, whom I have never known. What obedient child would doubt the hopeful tale of her father, a tale that her father himself believed? Besides, there never existed reason to doubt the authenticity of my legacy. As if the truth might be hidden in the tale, I committed to imagination my father's words.

From his stories I learned that my mother's name was Misao and that she was a beautiful princess. "As a young woman," my father often began, "Misao earned the reputation as one of the most sought-after women in Japan."

It took many years for this story of my father's to unfold and many more years for me to recognize it as my own. Each time he began the tale, a rush of feeling would overtake him. His voice would stammer, as if he were reliving each event, and I would become faint from holding my breath when he paused between words. Often my father would stop altogether. On such occasions I would encourage him to continue. "She wasn't like any of the other women, was she?"

"Misao was more beautiful," he'd say. "More learned in all of the arts." He'd sit at the foot of my bed and talk on and on until the language he spoke was no longer recognizable to my ear. When I could stand it no longer I would call his attention back to me.

"Where is Misao tonight?" I'd ask.

"She is visiting her mother in Japan," he would say. Or, "She is in a boat on her way home."

"That is why you must pray," my father said. "Pray for her safe return."

I could have spent my entire life praying. Still, I wondered, *Why had my mother failed to return?* The slightest speculation as to my mother's whereabouts filled my heart with the same foreboding that shook my father's voice when he spoke of her. "We must have patience," my father would say before turning out the light above my bed at night.

For my father's sake, I had patience.

I spent my childhood waiting patiently for my mother, certain that my own destiny depended on her return. It wasn't that I didn't love my father, only that the pain he endured was my own, a pain I felt with my heart.

It was for my father that I began meeting the ships that arrived from time to time carrying passengers from Japan. I dressed in fine clothes and waited alone on the docks for my mother. I recalled the story of Urashima

Taro, the young man who left his home for a long journey, only to find that no one recognized him when he returned. I would know my mother when I saw her. Her clothes would not be soiled like other women's. She would not appear frail or sickly. I would know my mother by her beauty, the same robust beauty that my father claimed I had inherited. I would recognize my mother and I would be there to show her the way home in case she had forgotten.

A ship arriving from Japan was a big event. Japanese from all over California went to the docks to wait for relatives or friends. Sometimes young men would carry pictures to identify a bride that had been chosen for them in Japan. Those men were the most impatient. I could not help but giggle at the way they pushed and crowded one another, each wanting to be the first in line when the gate swung open. I marveled at their expressions, twisted between fear and joy, their eyes peered into the distance, beads of sweat accumulated on their foreheads even in the mildest weather. When the ferry loaded with immigrants pulled away from Angel Island, a cheer would swell the crowd and handkerchiefs would begin to wave. The women would murmur excitedly among themselves and the men would clear their throats to ready themselves for words. But as the ferry docked, a silence would fall over the crowd. Perhaps everyone wondered what would happen if the person they had come to greet did not appear.

In the time it took the ferry to dock, a million sensations scattered my thoughts. First the salt air, like so many tears, and then the stronger smell of disinfectant and other, stranger odors. A mass of black heads bobbed close to the railing, and the monotonous, even cadence of spoken Japanese sailed through the air. In a moment of utter uncertainty, I bit my lip to hold back tears.

The passengers, as they moved past me, smelled of disinfectants mixed with the stench of sickness and the more subtle odor of fatigue. Usually the women's hair was cropped unfashionably short. Their dresses were often torn and stained. Could my mother be among such a group of women? I watched for her. As masses of bodies deadened my sight, I alone waited. The hem of a woman's dress might brush my face, a suitcase might knock against my arm, a careless foot might scuff my shoe, but my face remained unclaimed.

On the docks there was no room for fantasy. So why did I return to greet each ship? It was on the docks that I realized a sadness I had never known. On the docks that I' began to hate my mother.

I am said to be the daughter of a Japanese princess, though my life has been nothing like a fairy tale. The truth is that my mother is the cause of my sorrow. Perhaps it is not right for a daughter to admit to such feelings for her mother. Still, there is a pain in my heart which will not allow me to keep silent. The doctors tell me not to worry, but I doubt I will live much longer.

If my mother had taken care of my father, perhaps he would not have died at such a young age. It is a pity to think that my father left so many dreams unfulfilled. As a young man, he had ambition and the talent necessary to become a great physician. In San Francisco he did the best he could, but when petty obstacles prevented him from obtaining the title of doctor, he invested in a barbershop and learned to cut hair with the care and precision of a master surgeon repairing a lung or a heart. Unlike my father, the Japanese who immigrated to California while I was growing up were not professionals. Kuwata was a poor farmer, Mitsui a factory worker, Yawada a common houseboy; they came to the West with great hopes, but they possessed neither money nor skills, and too often hakujins failed to distinguish my father from them. Once, my father took me shopping downtown to a restaurant owned by hakujins and the waiter refused to serve us lunch. A man of great dignity, my father never spoke of that incident, but it caused him embarrassment, and after that I watched the coarse mannerisms of other Japanese very carefully and kept to myself whenever possible.

It seems to me now that my father must have foreseen his untimely death. In 1916, the year I was to graduate from high school, he wrote to a reliable marriage broker in Japan to express his concern over finding me a suitable husband. I remember greeting Isamu from the same dock on which I had stood awaiting the return of my mother, though my thoughts that day were not for her. It was an exceptionally sunny, mild day. I remember it well because even more radiant than the sun's light was Isamu, the handsomest man to step off the *Tohu Maru*. Aside from my father, there seemed no better man than Isamu, and each morning after his arrival he accompanied my father to his barber shop for training. Within a year, Isamu and I were married.

In choosing a match for me, my father used the same care that earned him the respect of all who knew him. Only the most respectable Japanese had shops on Grant Street, a prominent meeting place in the heart of the city, and of these family-run businesses my father's barbershop was the busiest. Kimura owned a shoe repair, Ueda ran a teahouse, and Ikemoto had a flower shop, but of all the proprietors, my father alone was admired by all. Because he possessed great skill as a barber, his reputation was established in the Japanese community not only on fine hairstyles, but also by those who came to him seeking advice, or troubled by a bodily disorder. From all over the city, people seemed to flock to my father, who was as adept at settling disputes as he was at pulling a bad tooth or removing an unsightly mole.

My father's death was indeed a great tragedy. Over two hundred people came to offer condolences at his funeral, and conciliatory offerings were sent, even from people whose names I'd never before heard.

I felt it my personal duty to see that the memorial

service ran smoothly, and therefore I spared no expense. I had Ikemoto send dozens of the freshest orchids and lilies. I even ordered trays of refreshments for the guests who attended. It was only natural that my husband Isamu, who had so recently arrived from Japan, would find fault with my way of conducting the funeral. "A Japanese funeral must not be handled like a party," he criticized. I had to take him aside and explain to him that things are simply different here, in America.

As it turned out, the arrangements for my father's funeral had so consumed me that when the time came for me to rise and deliver the eulogy, I did not feel sad. I was too busy counting the black heads, those faces that appeared in every corner, more than I had expected. I wondered if there would be enough refreshments; perhaps my choice of orchids had not been quite right. Nevertheless, I managed to make the best of circumstances, fulfilling, as I saw fit, my filial responsibilities.

Even given the respect he felt for my father, my first husband Isamu could not make up for my loss. Part of the problem, I suppose, was that Isamu spoke very little English. Because the introductory letter my father received from the marriage broker stated that Isamu had studied English at Tokyo University, I was certain that he understood more than he would reveal. Often, he refused to construct the simplest phrase. When only a word or two might be required, he would appear addled, disoriented, a trait that I fear his offspring inherited. But, of course, our daughter Rio was only an infant at the time.

When I think of it, English always posed a problem for Isamu—even the simplest command. Stop for manju on your way home from work, I would tell him. And it wasn't that he forgot, forgetfulness could be understood. Instead, he would arrive back with things I didn't even need. If I hadn't known better, I would have mistaken my husband for an idiot.

Although I could have spoken to Isamu in Japanese, this is America. Had I allowed him to use Japanese instead of English, how would he ever have learned? His mind would have grown feeble, and I have always believed what my father taught me—that a lazy mind cannot be tolerated. But perhaps I was too severe with Isamu. After all, it isn't that I can't speak Japanese.

Beginning as a young girl, I attended Japanese language class every day after school. I practiced my kana nightly, using the same methods by which I had memorized the letters of the English alphabet. I have fond memories of Japanese class. It was nothing like the public elementary school I attended where each student was treated like the next, without regard to family status or individual merit. In Japanese school, my teachers showed me favor by adding the honorific -sama to the end of my name, while

referring to other students simply as -san. In turn, I earned
the respect of my teachers by my ability to learn and by
the good manners taught me by my father. I am proud
that my father raised me according to Japanese tradition,
even though I have never set foot in Japan.

It was in my eighth year that I met Aiko, the daughter
of Ueda-san, the tea shop owner. Aiko was a curious girl.
Unlike me, she did not seem to care about her studies or
what people thought of her. When I walked down the
street, people could not fail to notice my good carriage,
but Aiko dressed and acted like a boy. At first I felt only
disgust for her. Though she and I attended the same elementary school, I did not befriend her for fear that being
seen in her company would blemish my reputation. But in
the afternoon Aiko and I attended Japanese school together and one evening as I began my walk home Aiko's
mother called me aside and introduced herself. I had seen
Mrs. Ueda before, but I would never have recognized her
as Aiko's mother. Unlike Aiko, the woman I had noticed
standing just beyond the school gate was beautiful. She
should have been my mother, not Aiko's—her skin was as
clear as mine and she had the same long, slender neck and
tall nose. I was surprised when she called my name, and,
having been taught to respect my elders, I could find no
way to refuse her invitation to visit the Ueda home.

On a Saturday afternoon in early May I walked with
Mrs. Ueda and Aiko downtown to the Ueda home, which

was located behind the family-owned tea shop. In the kitchen a single light bulb which hung from the ceiling made the room appear dirty for lack of daylight, and not more than five feet away another set of curtains parted into a darkened hallway. Standing near the door waiting for Aiko to bring me into the sitting room I noticed that the air smelled fleshy; perhaps it was the odor of day-old rice, and I began to feel dizzy. Just then two boys slightly older than Aiko and myself galloped into the room. Mrs. Ueda smiled. "These are my sons. Hitoshi is my oldest, and my middle boy is Yuichi.

"Please excuse my messy kitchen," she added, without the slightest pause between two such incongruous thoughts.

The beautiful woman who was Aiko's mother moved quickly around the cramped kitchen and in a few minutes she had prepared a snack consisting of Japanese tea cakes and fruit juice and was motioning to Aiko and me with her arms. "Please sit down," she said. "It's not much, but I hope you will enjoy it."

Aiko ate greedily, without looking up. As she chewed her tea cake Hitoshi and Yuichi ran around the table noisily, pretending to be pirates, but Mrs. Ueda's silence had the effect of making me feel as if she and I were alone in the room. I could not meet her eyes, though her gaze pierced my skin. In the sugary fruit juice I tasted her embarrassment and I drank it down with my eyes shut picturing the pink path it traced to my stomach. Mrs. Ueda watched me and I wanted to say something, but I could not trust my tongue to speak.

Hitoshi was the one to break the silence. His black eyes darted from Aiko to me until finally he began. "Aiko, is this the friend you've been bragging about?"

Aiko's face reddened. She opened her mouth exposing half-chewed tea cake and Hitoshi gripped his sides with laughter. Mrs. Ueda held the white ends of her apron to her mouth. Then she spoke to her daughter in a low, angry voice. "Go to your room, Aiko."

In the same instant Hitoshi's black eyes glared up at me with an intensity I mistook for hatred. I would never have believed then that the elder Ueda son would become my second husband. "You too," Mrs. Ueda commanded Hitoshi. "Since you cannot mind your manners, please leave the room now."

When Aiko and her brother had vanished, Mrs. Ueda directed her conversation at me. "We are not a bad family, though it may seem that way," she told me. "We have met with unfortunate circumstances here in San Francisco, but I would like Aiko to become as well-mannered and learned as you. Perhaps you would be kind enough to tutor her. Her hiragana teacher says she daydreams in class, and I would like your help to save her from the disgrace of lagging behind."

A great burden had been placed in my hands that

afternoon, but I could not refuse Mrs. Ueda's request. Never before had another person's learning been placed in my care, and because Aiko's studies had been entrusted to me, I put great effort into being a responsible teacher. On a cloudy morning in June, I brought Aiko home for her first tutoring session. My house is near the top of Nob Hill, and when Aiko stopped to catch her breath in front of it, I assumed she had become winded from the climb. But she continued to stare as if she did not believe it was real. "It's blue, isn't it," she exclaimed.

I followed her gaze to the house; that its color was blue had never before concerned me.

"It's like the ocean," she continued, "with cloud-colored trim."

Aiko had a way of making even the most trivial qualities of the house seem noteworthy. She began calling it the "dream house." Like my father, she felt most comfortable in the kitchen, where her gaze would travel out the window to the city far below. But my father's reasons for daydreaming were different. He had a habit of rising before the sun, and before fixing breakfast he'd sit at the kitchen table waiting for the first band of light to appear across the horizon. On sunny mornings rays of light would bounce off the water and provide enough light for him to cook by. But on foggy mornings my father planted himself beside the window, a lamp of darkness, and gazed motionless through the gray shadows. My father used to say that people ought to be able to stare through darkness, to recognize motion and sound like cats. But the truth is that my father was thinking about my mother at those times; like a cat in the darkness he was trying to locate her.

I found that by forcing Aiko to sit with her back to the window she accomplished a great deal. She was a bit dull, as one might have expected, but by fall I had managed to teach her the phonetic alphabet for both Japanese and foreign words.

One day, with dictionary in hand, I endeavored to show Aiko how to print the characters for her name. Once she had mastered the strokes, I explained that the ai- of Aiko means love.

"My own name has several meanings," I continued. "Depending on the character you choose, rei- can signify proper etiquette or it can show a clear mind. It also means beautiful."

Aiko was fascinated by the Japanese characters. By the end of the afternoon, she had gone through the members of her family so that her list of kanji extended practically to the bottom of the page. After printing the variations of my own name, followed by my father's name Tsuyoshi, meaning strength, I printed the character found in the dictionary under chastity.

"Misao," Aiko surmised. "Who is that?"

"My mother," I said. But without even looking up I knew it was too late. I could not take back my words.

Aiko blurted out, "You don't have a mother."

"Of course I do." I scolded her, unable to conceal my pain.

"Then where is she?" Aiko pressed.

She's visiting her mother in Japan. I could not tell her that. *She's in a boat, on her way home.* Responses that had always sounded believable coming from my father's lips were truths I dared not utter.

The room fell silent. I wanted to punish Aiko for her petulance. Still, I could think of nothing that would hurt her the way I had been wounded. "Of course you know my mother is a princess," I began, almost before I could know what had been said.

I concentrated on the character Misao as I spoke, but out of the corner of my eye I saw Aiko's curious face. "If you want me to tell you about her, you must promise not to repeat what I say to you."

Aiko offered her pinky from across the table and I hooked it in mine.

"It so happens that my mother was a princess," I began. "The most beautiful in Japan.

"She had to leave San Francisco because the climate here was too harsh for her. She has very delicate skin and dampness does not agree with her."

Aiko's eyes remained fixed on me, but at the mention of "delicate skin" I could see her top lip curl.

"Actually," I paused, "my mother didn't want to return to Japan, but my father saw that she was suffering here. A princess cannot be expected to live without the many servants and luxuries she is accustomed to. Besides, she missed her family, who, because they were royalty, could not leave Japan. It was my father who decided that my mother should return to Japan to visit her family.

"She missed her family," I repeated, not because I knew this to be true, but because I was moved by these words that I'd heard so many times from my father's lips. "She missed them so much," I said with a sigh.

When I had finished my story, I brought Aiko into our living room, where a glass case held an ornamental Japanese doll dressed in traditional kimono. "See," I said, "this doll was made as a gift for my mother."

"You're lying," she said.

"One day soon my mother will return, perhaps with her entire royal family to accompany her.

"Cross my heart," I told her, though suddenly I hated Aiko for making me swear to things that were none of her business. She was, after all, practically a stranger and telling her about my mother had done nothing to benefit me. Aiko would go on to achieve the highest marks in school because of me, yet already I felt her betrayal. Because of that afternoon, I could never consider Aiko my true friend. I felt only hatred toward Aiko, for the story she had made me tell.

I might not have missed my mother at all if her absence had not caused my father such sorrow. My father's gaze in the morning was like the steely needle of a compass, forever pointing east, never faltering from its course. I know this because I grew up watching my father, feeling his sorrow, imagining too that I knew his every thought, the way I assumed he knew mine. But of course I was wrong. Gone with my father was an accumulation of factual information I could not have known, knowledge that would tell me how to go on.

I was lost without my father. For a time after his death, I even considered leaving San Francisco for Japan. In the morning, I would sit in his chair in the kitchen, trying to make a plan as the sun gave light to the horizon. But each minute only broadened my sorrow.

When I told Isamu of my fantasy, he was elated. He bragged about the advantages Japan could offer him as a Japanese citizen, advantages from which I too would benefit, he claimed, even though I was born in San Francisco.

It was while I listened to Isamu boast that I began to realize the impossibility of my ever setting foot in Japan. At first I merely complained, "I am not fond of ocean travel, or any type of travel for that matter."

When that wouldn't satisfy him, I argued, "Japan is not my home. San Francisco is where I grew up." To myself I added: This house has survived earthquake, fire, flood, my father's death, I want it to be the house where I too will die.

For the same reason that I had not been able to satisfy Aiko with my stories, I could not explain to Isamu why I had to stay in America, not leave my home for Japan; it was the same reason it had never occurred to me as a child that I might simply set sail to Japan in order to be with my mother. Without my father, with memory alone to serve me, how would I have known my mother? Would I have recognized her? Perhaps we would pass on the street like two strangers. Such a thought haunted me.

Still, I might have returned to Japan with my family had Isamu not grown weak after my father's death. Although it was expected that he would run my father's barbershop, it soon became evident that my husband could not take my father's place. Isamu had even less skill as a barber than he had speaking English. Any amount of questioning about the daily activity of running the barbershop would lead to the same perfunctory reply. "Not bad," he would say. "About the same as yesterday."

"Don't worry," he cautioned me.

I worried constantly. For as long as I could remember, my father had always opened his shop promptly at eight o'clock, but Isamu was no good in the morning. He was no better than the baby, who would sleep until I woke her. The worst part of the morning was seeing Isamu across the kitchen table dressed in my father's waistcoat. No matter how thoroughly I laundered it, it never came clean. It never fit him properly either. It sagged across his chest and tended to wrinkle the moment he touched it.

But perhaps I speak too severely of Isamu. I did, after

all, pity him. Evenings after dinner while I manicured his nails, I recalled how my father's hands had always been a source of great pride to me. Compared to my father, who kept his hands meticulously clean and buffed his nails until the white moons shone, Isamu's hands were a disgrace. At the end of the day his nails looked as if he'd spent all day biting them. And always at least half a dozen cuts and scratches appeared up and down his wrists. Still, it seemed that no matter how much I pitied my husband and no matter how much I questioned or scolded, matters did not improve.

Perhaps I was too harsh on Isamu, but I have no regrets. I did the best I could, given the circumstances. I was grieving for my father, whom I had loved my whole life, yet for all appearances Isamu was the one who appeared to be deep in mourning.

Even as a small child, I would go with my father to his shop, where I would sit behind the counter for hours watching him. There the fresh smell of castile soap blended with rich hair oils and fragrant cigars. I loved my father's barbershop for its brilliant colors: spritzer bottles tinted deep sea blue, forest green shampoos, the fiery orange of iodine.

From my position behind the counter, I would watch the reflection of men lined four in a row with white aprons wrapped across their chests like dinner napkins. I can still hear the crack of the apron as my father shook it out, see the way it billowed in the air and then settled as my father tied the ends into a neat knot.

My father's barbershop was the only place in town where Yamamoto, who worked in Folger's coffee factory, would be seated beside Inamura, the gardener, and beside him Ikemoto, who owned the flower shop. And it seemed that no matter where conversation began, talk would inevitably wander to the subject of women. Since there were very few Japanese women in San Francisco, men would often come to my father with sample pictures from Japan, to ask his advice over which woman they ought to choose for a bride. A month or two later they would return, proud of their selection.

Once Inamura arrived with pictures and became so excited that he wound up staying the entire afternoon. I remember him well because he was bald. My father would smear head wax between his hands and then buff Inamura's scalp the way he did the brass signpost outside his shop. Even after he married, Inamura continued to seek my father's advice.

At those times, so as not to be intrusive, I would flip through the stacks of Japanese magazines that my father kept behind the counter. I could tell immediately the ones with pretty Japanese women inside, because those pages would reveal tiny creases, just like skin, from excessive handling.

One day I had the idea to return to my father's shop. More than a year had elapsed since my father's death and it occurred to me that I had avoided not only the shop but all of Grant Street as well in the year since Isamu had taken over. After a period of mourning, my head was again filled with nostalgia over the time I'd spent with my father there as a child. But when I returned to my father's shop, I was surprised to find that it was as quiet as a morgue. I could not remember a time when all four seats had not been filled, yet there was only one customer, only the faintest snip-snip of scissors. It was so quiet you could hear hair brushing the ground.

Though I thought I knew all my father's customers, I did not recognize the man in the chair that day and Isamu did not introduce me. My own husband only nodded to me in the mirror, then continued his work in silence.

It is fortunate that my father raised me to be so independent in my actions. Another woman, unable to bear the grief I felt that day, might have given up hope. A weaker woman might have resigned herself to letting her life be ruined. But I have no tolerance for weakness in myself or others. The business would have collapsed had I left it in Isamu's hands.

I can still recall the strength of my determination when I sat Rio in the kitchen for her first haircut. She couldn't have been more than two years old, but the fact that she had a head full of hair worked to my advantage. I trimmed just an inch at first, blunt across the bottom. Then I layered it like a Christmas tree. Finally, gathering confidence, I cut above the ears, in a style I would need to perfect with practice. But my daughter turned out to be the worst customer a barber could ask for. She kept sliding around on the chair, so that finally I had to belt her shoulders to keep her upright. Perhaps it was the sound of my snipping close to the ear that made her head shake from side to side, but how she struggled that day! I had to approach her with the care one would take to handle a wild animal; still, all the years of watching my father did not go to waste. In the end, I was satisfied with my results. Though even as her mother I could not say she was an attractive child, the haircut seemed to flatten her thick cheeks, and I was satisfied.

I thought that Isamu would understand my plan when he saw his daughter that night. Secretly, it was my hope that he would try to stop me. Rio would run into her father's arms, the way that was her habit when Isamu arrived home at the end of the day. I expected then that Isamu would react. I imagined his face growing pale with rage at the sight of his daughter, her hair cropped short like a boy. But Isamu simply pressed Rio's cheek tenderly to his, the way that was his habit when greeting her at the end of the day.

That night, no later than usual, I sat across the couch

from Isamu as he reclined with a book. I checked his eyes, certain that he could not be concentrating. Surely, I thought, he must be brooding. Out of courtesy to my husband, I waited for him to address me. I waited until finally I could wait no longer. "My father had great hopes of you taking over his business," I began.

To this, Isamu only screwed his eyes up at me. "Don't worry," he said.

"Do you remember your last words to my father?" I asked.

Isamu lay his book flat across his chest. "I promised to take care of his daughter, my wife."

"You are no more worthy of me than the lowliest of peasants," I retorted.

Isamu made no reply. It was without protest from my husband that I would carry out my plan, for my father's sake that I did what needed to be done. Yet deep in my heart I still begrudge Isamu for giving up so easily.

It has since occurred to me that mourning my father was to Isamu a way to prepare for his own death. It began at my father's funeral when he asked me what I believed happened to the spirit of the dead. Having been raised according to Confucian ethics, I had never concerned myself with such a question. "There is enough to be done in this life, let alone speculate over what cannot be known," I told my husband.

But Isamu's morbidity did not find relief in my answer. His fascination with death continued, until, as might have been expected, he no longer cared about life.

If I was harsh on Isamu, I have no regrets. I did what I could to stir the life in him. What else beside my desire to force Isamu into action could have inspired my plan to take over my father's barbershop?

I was willing to try anything, it seems, but in the end Isamu could not be helped. If my husband had complained of anything at all, I might have been able to ascertain what was wrong. But Isamu never complained. He only grew weaker and slept longer hours until one morning he failed to wake up altogether.

A weak woman would not have survived the death of her father, followed so soon by the death of her husband. Yet, I must say now that Isamu's death was indeed a terrible mystery. It set my heart racing in such a panic that to this day I have not recovered. Because I cannot know what form of illness caused my husband's death, I worry for myself and for my daughter Rio. Still, the thing to be done was to make the appropriate arrangements to have the body removed from the house. Thanks to my presence of mind, even under such circumstances, I was able to act quickly and carry out the first task by the end of the day. It was only afterward that a terrible panic filled my heart.

The night Isamu died, I sat alone in the living room

long after Rio lay asleep. That night a chill shook my heart so violently that I could not be still. Finally, I made up my mind to light a fire. Before that night the fireplace had never been used, though a stack of pine wood lay neatly to one side. And perhaps because the wood had been there for as long as I could remember, I regretted at first having to destroy it. Like everything in the house, the wood itself seemed to belong to my father. Once placed by his strong hands, it provided me with memory.

But slowly, as the flames leaped high into the air, the fire's heat overtook me. I recalled the way Isamu looked when he stepped off the *Tobu Maru*, not four years before his death. He was the handsomest man I had ever seen. When the fire threatened to die I fed it logs; in that way I was able to forget the passage of time. I felt mesmerized by the shadowy dance of blues and greens, seduced by the orange that shot up into yellow-white light.

Gathering Isamu's belongings from his drawers, I piled them into stacks and lined the front of the fireplace. Then, one by one, I disposed of every trace of my husband's illness. I wanted to remember Isamu as he was, not the way death had changed him—how my own life had changed until all that remained was Rio and myself.

It was near the bottom of the last stack of Isamu's shirts that I came across a note written in my husband's script. "To my wife Reiko," it said. "Please take a picture of Rio and send it with my ashes to my parents in Japan."

Had I known Isamu's wishes before I disposed of his body I would, of course, have reacted accordingly. Still, what difference could it have made? The next day I took Rio to Ben Shimada, the man who is still considered to be the finest photographer in San Francisco. To mark the occasion I dressed my daughter in lace and white stockings. What a pity that even the best clothing could not make her beautiful! Watching her squint into the camera I had a premonition of my own death.

Before Rio was born I counted the important events of my life by the ships that docked in San Francisco Bay. Since my daughter's birth the passage of my life has been marked only by disaster. Still, I did not lose sight of my obligation. In fulfillment of my husband's request I sent Rio's photograph to Japan along with a sealed urn.

From Water
You Come

1
·
N o m i

The house where I live with my mother, Grandma Rio, and Granny Reiko looks like the Japanese word for gossip. I know this because Granny Reiko showed me how to draw it. First you make the three women: Granny Reiko who is my great-grandmother, and my mother, and below them Grandma Rio. You draw them sitting down, as close together as you can without making them touch. Then you put the roof over their heads, which Granny Reiko says belongs to her and keeps them inside. Even though I am seven years old and already in the second grade, I am not part of this picture, and neither is my older sister Melodie, and when I asked Granny Reiko why, she gave me an answer I don't understand. It took her a long time to say anything, long enough to make me think I probably shouldn't have asked; then she held my chin up so that my neck was stretched way back and we were looking straight at each other. "What is gossip without sound?" she said. Then she shut her eyes in a way that let me know I should leave her room.

My mother calls Granny Reiko unpredictable. That means I'm not supposed to ask her questions or if she tells me something it might not be the truth. I went upstairs to ask her to teach me a Japanese word because tomorrow each of us is supposed to bring a foreign word to class and my mother said she couldn't think of a good one, but even though Granny has given me a word I'm afraid it isn't right. My mother says gossip is when you talk bad about other people and that isn't a nice thing to do, so I don't understand why the word for gossip looks like our house, except that my mother and Grandma Rio both say that Granny is not a nice person. Still, I don't know what I will do tomorrow when everyone brings a new word and I am the only one with nothing.

I went downstairs to ask Grandma Rio what I should do because she is very smart, but this time she couldn't help me. First she said she couldn't open her eyes because they hurt too much. Then when I brought her a Kleenex to wipe away the ooze she gets sometimes when she sleeps too much, and she put on her glasses and held up her magnifying glass and looked at the paper where Granny Reiko had printed the word for gossip, she couldn't even read it. "What is this, anyway?" she said.

"It's Mommy and Granny and you, and there's the

roof, see?" I had to point because Grandma is nearsighted, which means she's practically blind.

"What's wrong with Granny?" Grandma closed her eyes, the same way Granny had, only I could tell she didn't want me to go. She laid the magnifying glass down beside her and squeezed my hand. "It's okay, Nomi," she said. And I knew then that I was wrong to have asked her for help. My mother told me Grandma wasn't feeling well and that I shouldn't bother her, and now there is going to be trouble.

The clock says it's almost midnight but I can't sleep. I know I should feel bad about going to see Grandma when my mother told me not to, but tomorrow is almost here and I don't have a word I can show anyone. If I bring the Japanese word for gossip everyone will laugh at me. They will see my house with my mother and great-grandmother and grandmother and they will think it's funny. Maybe I should have asked Grandpa Tadashi for a word, but Mommy says Grandpa Tadashi is not the right person to ask about words. He likes plants and flowers and the fish he raises in the pond in our backyard, and that's why he stays outside so much. I wanted to ask my father, but he doesn't like being interrupted when he's writing his sermons on Thursday nights, and he never finishes till after I'm asleep, and I have to go to bed at eight. If I get out of bed now my mother will get mad. She'll ask why I'm not asleep, but she won't listen if I try to tell her. She'll say, If you're not in bed and asleep in the next thirty seconds there's going to be big trouble.

Through the wall I can hear her talking. She and my father must be in the kitchen, which is past my sister's room and down the hall, but my mother has a big voice. "I'm telling you I don't know what we're going to do about her," she is saying, and I know she is talking about me. I put the pillow over my head because this voice of my mother's scares me, but even then I can't not hear her. As she talks I try to make myself shrink smaller and smaller. I cover my head and neck with the pillow, then slide the sheet up over my body and under my hands and feet until no part of me is sticking out. I am trying to disappear, but my mother's voice keeps getting louder. Maybe my father is saying something too, but I can't hear him. I only hear my mother, closer and closer and now footsteps. "You're not here during the day so you can't tell me. You're going to have to do something." When the footsteps stop just outside my door a buzzing fills my head like bees inside my ears and the next thing I know it is morning.

I don't want to cause more trouble, but at breakfast things are still not right. Usually my mother asks my sister and me how we slept. She pours our milk and cereal for us and watches while we eat and drink so we don't spill. But this morning you can tell it is not going to be a good day by the way she rushes my sister and me. I don't spill a drop of milk on the table or on my lap, only I can't seem to eat fast enough. Hurry, hurry, my mother's eyes say. Why are you so slow? When I open my closet I pick the first dress my hand touches and do not forget to brush my teeth and hair and when I'm ready to go even before my older sister and almost even before my mother has my lunch ready I sit waiting quietly, hoping my mother will notice and not be angry anymore.

At eight-fifteen the three of us walk down to the garage, so that my mother can drive Melodie and me to school, only this morning the car will not start. The engine makes a coughing sound, then it becomes quiet again. For a minute my mother sits perfectly still. She turns over her shoulder and stares at us in the back seat, the way she does when we've done something wrong. "You two are going to be late."

I have never been late to school. I look from my mother to Melodie, who seems as puzzled as me.

"You'd better walk."

I am in the second grade, but it has never occurred to me that it is possible to walk to school.

"You're big girls now."

"But we'll be late," Melodie says.

"Just tell your teachers what happened," says my mother. "They'll understand."

My whole hand clasped tightly in Melodie's, I fly down the hill that leads away from home. With my head turned, I watch my mother disappear feet first, then hips, then shoulders until all that remains is a waving hand that seems to call me back. *Tell the teacher what happened. You're big girls now.* I repeat my mother's words carefully in my head. What could she possibly mean?

I don't know why my mother is making me walk to school. Melodie will always be the only big girl in our family. "Come on, Nomi," she commands me. "Turn your head around. Faster, faster."

On the corner a big red sign with white letters says STOP. My mother has taught us what to do when we see that sign. Stand on the curb and look both ways and then if there aren't any cars coming walk across the street. *Don't run.* I don't want to run out into the street, but Melodie pulls me off the curb. I want to obey my mother but my feet move beneath me even faster than Melodie's. My lunch pail feels heavy in my hand. It slaps against my leg and I can hear the thermos clanking inside and a car passing us—*Those children are going to be on time*—and the street winds slowly down the hill so that between the houses and trees I can see the bay, and it's so sunny out that the water looks like tinfoil, and even though I can't see it, I know that the school isn't far away and we are going to be late.

Melodie leaves me breathless at the door to my classroom, which is on the way to hers. She lets go of my hand, and, holding her lunch pail between her legs, wipes her palms across my face. "Don't be a crybaby," she says. "See? We aren't late." She points through the window at the clock, which reads twenty-eight minutes after eight. There are still two minutes before the late bell. I want to tell Melodie I'm not a crybaby, but I touch my hands to my cheeks and they are sticky and wet. I watch Melodie run down the corridor until suddenly she disappears. The rows of tan-colored walls and blue doorways have swallowed my sister and left me standing outside my classroom alone.

Mrs. Bean stands in front of the blackboard; she doesn't notice that I am not in my seat, or know that I have flown like a flying fish behind my sister to get to school. She doesn't know that on this day my mother has called me a big girl and refused to take me to school. *You're a big girl now,* she said. *Tell the teacher, she'll understand.* I can't tell the teacher that.

At recess I look for my sister on the playground. When I see her playing dodgeball I run up to the court and sit down on the gray cement. A couple of times I think she sees me so I wave, but Melodie doesn't pay any attention. She is my sister and at night I can hear when she cries because she sleeps in the room next to mine, and once we even had the same nightmare. But now, when she is standing so close, it is as if she is someone else. She aims the big red ball at the boys and most of the time it hits them. Then she jumps up and down and takes her place inside the court and sticks out her tongue and scrunches up her face daring them to hit her back.

When the bell rings to tell us it's time to go back to class I run onto the court and tap Melodie's shoulder. "Do you know a foreign word I can bring to class?"

Melodie carries the dodgeball under one arm. She stops and bounces it to me. "How about our last name?"

"What does it mean?" I bounce it back.

"Hito. H-I-T-O. It means 'person.'" Melodie tucks the ball back under her arm and slices the air with her index finger to show me the character. "Mommy taught me," she brags.

If Hito means person, I wonder if my friends' names, like Sutterfield and Smith, have secret meanings too? Maybe Melodie is lying and Hito doesn't mean anything at all, but she was in Mrs. Bean's class last year and Mrs. Bean thinks she is very smart.

You can tell whether or not Mrs. Bean thinks you're smart when she calls on you. She'll get a funny look on her face, or speak too slow, or turn her head to one side. She likes Rosemary and April and most of the boys, but she has a special face reserved just for me. It says, I know you have the right answer so don't disappoint me.

Manuel Diaz recites the numbers up to ten in Spanish. "Uno, dos, tres, quatro, cinco, seis, siete, ocho, nueve, diez," and when he finishes Mrs. Bean claps her hands.

Then she makes everyone repeat them after him. Next she calls on Rosemary, who stands up and says, "Sombrero, that means hat in Mexican." "Spanish," Mrs. Bean corrects her. "Thank you, Rosemary." Everyone knows how to count to ten in Spanish, and when my name is called, I am thinking what a simple word sombrero is, *how stupid*, but when I stand up and look at Mrs. Bean my word won't come out. "Nomi"—she repeats my name—"go ahead, please."

"Hito." I say, feeling the blood pounding in my ears. "H-I-T-O. It means person in Japanese."

"Isn't that your last name, Nomi?"

"Yes."

"Then this must have been a very easy assignment for you."

Rosemary giggles.

"Yes," I lie.

"Do you know what your first name means?"

"Yes," I lie again.

"What does it mean?"

I shrug my shoulders.

Mrs. Bean frowns. She waits before saying anything. Then she says, "Thank you, Nomi. You may sit down."

At the end of the day I am the first one out the door. I am about to run to the gate to find my mother, but she catches me in the doorway and takes my hand. "Let's go get Melodie." She greets me without a smile or hello, which makes me think she is still angry, but I feel safe walking beside her. Melodie is almost to the gate when we catch up with her. We call her name, and when she turns around she too looks relieved. Now we can walk back home, the way we came this morning, only this time the three of us. Then Melodie runs up ahead. "Our car," she points. Now I see it too.

"It was flooded this morning," my mother says.

"Flooded," I say. I think of Noah's ark floating on the ocean, but that's not right.

"Hurry now." My mother begins tugging at my arm. "Get in."

Once the car is moving, my mother speaks to us from over her shoulder. "Grandma Rio is in the hospital," she says.

"Why?" I ask.

When my mother doesn't respond immediately Melodie says, "Because she's sick, that's why people go to the hospital."

"That's why most people go to the hospital," my mother is talking again. "But there are other reasons too."

"Why?" I try again.

"Grandma tried to kill herself." My mother says these words slowly, the way Mrs. Bean talks when she thinks you don't know the answer, except she is not asking a question. Her words are serious, frightening. She waits for a moment, maybe because she doesn't want to scare us anymore, then she says, "You see, Grandma was very un-happy. Do you understand?"

I know I should say yes, but for what seems like a long time none of us says anything. My mother slows the car down when she approaches the STOP sign Melodie made me run past in the morning. Then, when the car stops moving, she turns over her shoulder and I can tell she feels sorry for us.

"Is Grandma going to die?" Melodie breaks the silence.

"She might."

"Can't the doctors do anything?"

"They are doing everything they can."

"Why did she want to kill herself?" I ask.

"We can't really know"—my mother pauses—"but I guess she didn't want to live anymore."

My mother is wrong about this. I go downstairs to visit Grandma Rio every day after school and she is always happy to see me. "She won't die, will she?" I am begging her to say no.

"We hope not. Daddy is at the hospital right now, and he should be able to tell you more when he gets home."

"What does she look like?" Melodie says.

"She looks like Grandma always looks," my mother says.

This answer makes me believe that things might not

be so bad after all because Grandma is beautiful. She has the palest skin and the blackest hair of anyone in our family, and even when she doesn't open her eyes, she smiles, and she holds my hand and asks me about my day and I can tell she is listening to every word I say. "When is she coming home?"

"We don't know yet."

Melodie and I sit on stools behind the counter while my mother cooks dinner and we want to know about Grandma again and again. *Is she going to die?* My mother doesn't like it when I keep asking the same questions, but things keep repeating in my head and sometimes I can't help saying them aloud. *Do you think Grandma will die? When will Grandma come home?* My mother tells Melodie and me that we should pray because God is the only one who can make Grandma safe, but I don't like to pray. I'd rather ask my mother.

As long as my mother keeps answering me it is possible to believe that Grandma will come home soon and everything will be fine. *She hasn't said we shouldn't ask,* but when my father gets back from the hospital his face says no more questions. His eyes are puffy and he won't look at me. He stands for a minute at the sink pouring himself a glass of water, but my mother has to turn off the faucet because he leaves it running, and then he stares into his glass and forgets to drink. When he reaches over to hug

Melodie and me he smells like the clothes my mother unpacks from the suitcase in my closet every fall. It is a dark, sour smell that sweaters get when you haven't worn them for a long time and that's why my mother shakes them over and over, then takes them outside for a day to hang in the sunshine. *Let them air!* she says. But it isn't just my father's clothes that smell funny. It's his skin when his cheek touches mine, and I am sure that this must be how death smells. *It's dark in there and there's no air, and that's why my mother has to take the sweaters outside where there's plenty of air and sunlight.* I rub my fingers through my hair, then I hold them under my nose and breathe in the smell of death.

"What have you girls been doing today?" My father thinks we don't know about Grandma.

Melodie and I roll our eyes at each other. "Nothing," she says.

"How is Grandma?" My mother wants him to tell us.

Daddy gives my mother a look that says *terrible.* Then he turns to us. "Not too bad."

"Come," my mother says, "let's have dinner."

"Grandpa's out back," my father says.

"Shall we call him in?"

"Sure."

"Nomi, why don't you go get him then."

It's still light outside, and the sky has a pink color that makes the half sun over the bay look big and red. As I walk along rows of fuchsia and ferns a warm breeze blows my hair back. I know I should be sad about Grandma, but I can't help feeling pretty in Grandpa's garden. There is plenty of air and all the bushes are green and trimmed just the way they should be.

At first I can't find Grandpa, but then I see the back of his white T-shirt. He is sitting on a stone beside his fishpond. I am about to call him, but something makes me keep walking and not say anything. When I get up close I can hear water trickling over the rocks and I can see that Grandpa Tadashi is holding a sheet of white paper in front of him and that his hands are shaking. I know it isn't right to watch him without his knowing, so I call him very softly and when he doesn't answer I watch the bubbles rising to the surface of the pond. Grandpa says the bubbles make it easier for the fish to breathe and you can tell it's true because the fish are bright red and blue and black and gold and white and they swim happily in and out of the bubbles. Once during the summer Grandpa's favorite fish Mica jumped out of the pond and landed in the branches of the sago palm. When Grandpa found Mica his gills were barely moving and his scales were dull and gray. My mother said Mica was going to die, but Grandpa put him into a tank all by himself with plenty of fresh water and then he sat with him all night and in the morning when I woke up Mica was swimming around with the other fish. Grandpa said that the soft branches of the sago palm shielded Mica from the sun and kept him damp, but my mother said that that just goes to show you that Grandpa can bring dead things back to life. Carefully, I step over the small pebbles that lead to the big stone where Grandpa sits and I put my arms around his neck. "Grandma is going to be all right," I whisper, half-pleading.

The skin on his neck is hard and warm beneath my fingertips, and Grandpa sits perfectly still. "It's okay, Nomi," he says, but I know it's not okay. I rub my hands across his shoulders and back the way my mother does to comfort me, and for a minute this seems to work. The muscles on Grandpa's back soften, and when his hands begin moving along my back I feel comforted too. We are both thinking about Grandma, wishing she could be here to see how pretty it is beside the pond with the bright-colored fish swimming in circles all around us.

Even with my back to the pond I can hear the bubbles and see the fish in my head, and now my heart is pounding in my ears and I can feel that it's not okay anymore. Grandpa misses Grandma even more than I miss her. And then all of a sudden his hands stop moving. It is quiet again and in the silence Grandpa moans like someone dying, and you can tell he loves Grandma most of all.

I am sorry for Grandpa, but sorrier for myself. I don't know how it is that I can go to sleep one night a second-grader and wake up the next morning a big girl.

The thing is, I don't look any different. In the bathroom, I climb up on my mother's white porcelain sink so that I can see my face in the mirror. I have the same brown eyes and long black hair I had the last time I checked, and the same new front teeth that my mother says are too big for my mouth. I am still Nomi Hito, only last night Grandma Rio was downstairs asleep in her room and tonight she is in the hospital, maybe she is even dead. A tear runs down my face and I stick out my tongue to catch it; the first one tastes bitter, but they get sweeter until their wetness is like milk. "Grandma," I mouth her name in the mirror, "do you know what I did today?"

I look down at my feet in the cold white sink. "No, Nomi, why don't you tell me."

"Today I became a big girl."

"And how did you do that?"

"I walked to school by myself."

"You did?"

"Yes, Mommy made me walk because she said that Melodie and I are big girls now. And Melodie taught me what our last name means. But the teacher wanted to know what my first name means."

"Nomi?" It's my mother's voice. "Nomi, what are you doing in there?"

"I'm brushing my teeth," I lie.

I climb down because I'm supposed to be getting ready for bed, but beneath the sink a bottle of Clorox catches my eye. I have seen it before; my mother uses it to clean the toilet. CAUTION, it says. I know that those bright red letters mean danger. THIS SUBSTANCE MAY BE FATAL IF SWALLOWED. I unscrew the blue bottle cap and touch it with the end of my tongue. It burns. I swallow and then I lie down on the cool tile floor with my eyes closed.

After a while my mother bangs on the door. "Nomi, what are you doing now?"

"Nothing."

"Come out then."

"I'll come out later."

"No," she says. "Come out now. It's time to go to bed."

That night as she pulls the sheet up to my neck my mother asks if I am upset about Grandma. "No," I lie.

"It's not your fault, you know."

It hasn't occurred to me that it is, but the instant she says these words I know I am to blame.

2

.

R i o

Mother waits. She does not call to ask how I am. She does not wonder, *How is Rio?* Or think, *Where is Rio?* I've heard talk that I've been here for two weeks, which I know to be two weeks longer than I have ever gone without seeing her. She was always there, even when I left home to get away from her. Still it does not occur to her that I am gone, that in the last two weeks I have wandered farther away than even I thought possible.

When I was a child, I dreamed of falling off the earth. I saw myself walking up the hill toward home—that old, blue house where I still live. I'd walk to the top of the hill, climb the sixteen steps that led to the front door, and on the other side would be nothing. I'd fall through the air as if through water. I'd sink lower and deeper, unable to breathe. As a child, the dream came routinely as a nightmare. Every muscle in my body would tighten and my teeth would rip away the inside of my cheek.

The real terror came when I'd wake up midflight in my bed as if I had never left it—that was where it all began and ended. But later I started to have the dream during the day. Walking down the hill, away from home, I would experience the weightlessness of my body. I would hold my breath as if to defy all that air around me saying, *Breathe, Breathe.* I would hold my breath until the wind did not exist. Then the pavement beneath me became nothing but the rhythmic treading of my feet slapping against it and the sky above me was neither gray nor blue but the red-black color of blood. I'd hold my breath until all that remained was the excruciating pain in my chest that felt like the purest pleasure I had ever known.

I never told anyone about that dream. First there was no one to tell, and then I must have just forgotten. Like it's been with everything else, I had to be reminded. I had to hear the hissing of the oxygen tank beside my bed, feel the air fed by tubes up my nostrils that says, *Breathe, Breathe.* Only now it is different. The pain is not pure, nor is it a thing I can make bearable on my own.

Tomoe stands beside my bed. My son's wife is my good mother. She is my nurse. She comes to my room when it is dark outside. She wears white, or pink, or yellow. She smells like a bunch of freshly cut gardenias. Her hands are not petal-soft, but callused and worthy of admiration. I want to absorb the strength of her touch, to mold my palm into hers.

Her voice sounds no different than it did eleven years ago when Goro brought her home. She has that same matter-of-fact, this-is-the-way-it-is tone of authority about her. I loved that quality of hers from the start. Even then I sensed she was capable in ways I couldn't imagine.

I still believe in Tomoe, without question, the way I always have, only now we share a mutual language. "Goro has the youth group tonight so he can't come." She is talking about my son. "Melodie and Nomi wanted me to tell you that they miss you." Now my grandchildren. "Tadashi is feeling a little better. He says he will be well enough to visit tomorrow." My husband. "I told Granny you're feeling a little better." She stops long enough for me to wonder, *Is she making excuses for me too?* Then she says, "Granny's been a real handful, you know." And I believe in her all over again.

Or perhaps it is only that I want to believe in Tomoe. I want to suck the air she breathes through my own lungs. I want her breath to heal me, but I am bound to the earth by two black straps and a row of silver bars to look out of. They are cold to the touch, and inflexible. They laugh at me. They say, *You will never escape.* I laugh back. They say, *Just try.* I laugh some more until I cannot remember why I began. Everywhere around me are signs of failure that point to why I am here. Wrapped around my wrist is a plastic bracelet that spells out my name as clearly as the word *defeat*. There is sickness stitched into the blanket that keeps me warm, sorrow on the face of the doctor who strides into the room to ask me what is so funny.

"You tell me," I say.

He leans over the bed rail, as if to reveal a secret. He says, "Do you know why you are here?"

I nod. I close my eyes. I dream that I am floating facedown on a bed of white lilies. It is almost a good dream, except that there are bees everywhere. They are hovering just above me, buzzing like a hacksaw in my ear. I cannot see them but I know that they are laying their eggs in the tangles of my hair. It is my fault, I know, because my hair has grown long and unruly. But my hair has not been long in years, and even in my dreams I know I am not a child anymore. I wake up thinking of my mother.

Granny's been causing trouble. Isn't that what Tomoe said? Granny was causing trouble even before she was Granny. Long before she became the great-grand-pain-in-the-ass that she's been to Tomoe's children she was Goro's out-of-control grandmother who locked him in the closet to teach him about life. She taught me about life, that's for sure. She is the mother to whom I owe everything, including the $537 balance remaining on the money I borrowed to have my hysterectomy ten years ago, in addition to another kind of balance I seem never to have possessed at

all. She was my mother before she was Goro's grandmother, and now she's Granny to the children. But she
was never just plain Reiko. Reiko was always the *princess*,
the spoiled daughter of a rich man who never had to lift a
finger. Look where that's gotten her . . . Look where it's
gotten me.

Why am I here? the doctor asks. Now that's a good
question. I can remember counting out twenty Percodan.
A dozen Tegratol, Valium, Codeine. Was that not enough?
I saved those pills. I spent more months than I can bear to
think about taking a quarter less than prescribed, sometimes half. I spent as many months planning for the day I'd
swallow them all down, in the morning, just after Tadashi
left the house. I couldn't do it with just one glass of water,
I remember that. I remember sitting on the edge of the
bed and holding up my magnifying glass so I could admire
the picture of Goro and my grandchildren, and then feeling along the nightstand to make sure the note I'd written
Tadashi was in a place where he could find it easily. I
swallowed a good fistful of pills then, but I needed more
water to finish them off so I got up and headed to the
bathroom, but in the hallway I had to turn back because I
forgot my glass, and then I couldn't see where I'd left the
vial of pills. By the time I swallowed them all and finally
lay down in bed I could feel the skin lifting off my bones.
That is where my memory ends. I want to feel that feeling
again but I have given up trying. It is daylight outside. A
night disguised by fluorescent white hospital lights has

turned into a day so bright that the space around me now
appears dim. Outside my window the leaves of some tall
sort of fig tree dance in the breeze. Even with my eyes
shut the leaf patterns keep flickering and the bed beneath
me becomes a raft. It moves swiftly past tall buildings on
one side and trees on the other. I have never seen this
type of scenery before but I know it leads to a waterfall,
and there is no way to stop the current. The sun beats
down on the thin gown I wear, which has become
drenched and transparent. I don't want people to see me
this way. I try to turn onto my stomach, but a hand grasps
my hand.

Tadashi hovers over me. He shakes his head. "You
were having a nightmare," he says.

I am dangling over the edge of the waterfall, waiting
to be released.

My husband presses his palm to my forehead. I want
to tell him to stop, but even before I realize that I am
irritated with him he sits down and the word *sorry* folds
over itself like a wave in my ear. I can feel the sweat that
covers my body like a stocking, see too that Tadashi's face
appears glossy and flushed. His chest looks swollen, as if
he is holding his breath. After twenty-eight years of marriage I can actually see words forming in his lungs. He
watches me, pensively, needing my permission to speak. I
watch as slowly he lets the air escape, until the surface
beneath me transforms into something stiff and solid.

Tadashi wipes his shirtsleeve across his forehead. He

looks tired, but not unlike himself. He tells me that he wanted never to say what he is going to say, but that he doesn't know what else he can do. He pauses.

I wait. I rode the raft, saw the fall approaching, but how could I have known I'd wind up here? He reminds me how, in the twenty-eight years of our marriage, he has never hurt me, never laid a hand on me in anger, never made me do anything I did not want to do.

I struggle to keep my eyes opened. I watch him gather himself upright. He has been faithful to me, he says. Faithfully he has worked hard to make me happy, loved me, cared for me, made sure I had a place to sleep and food to eat. He is saying all these things to me, he is right here beside my bed, but it is as if we are separated by water, stranded on opposite embankments. He says he cannot understand why I have done what I have done. He talks until there is no color left in his face, until my gaze retreats behind him where a yellow pitcher stands beside a pot of waxy red begonias.

He says he knows that people need to do things—or not do things. They know that those things will make others unhappy but they need to do those things anyway. He has tried to understand when I have done things that have hurt him, but he doesn't understand why I have done this. He looks at me hard, and I am certain he can see through blanket, sheet, nightgown, taste the bitter flesh he once held in his hands. Then, as if repelled, his eyes soften and I am left to wonder, *If he had gone farther, pene-trated through seven layers of skin and bone, what would he have seen?*

He says he has finished what he needed to say, he is sorry if his words have hurt me, but I know at once that he is not.

IF YOU COULD JUST TELL ME WHAT I HAVE DONE WRONG THEN MAYBE I CAN MAKE THINGS RIGHT FOR YOU. I know he is making his voice loud, but it doesn't feel loud. Perhaps he doesn't remember saying this before, how in the hushed breaking of dawn he once said, *Don't you know that I would do anything for you?* On that morning he pulled the hair back from my temples until my lids shuttered closed. I remember the way he pressed his mouth against mine, forced my lips to part, then silenced with his tongue the words rising in my throat. I had dreamt that night that it was not Tadashi who held me. It was another man whose body I summoned in sleep, his eyes I saw when I awoke. I have tried to forget until now. How can I say to Tadashi that his mistake was really my mistake, the mistake I made in choosing him. Now the green line on the monitor beside my bed registers my heartbeat like a Richter scale and I know that each breath carries with it a measured disaster. My husband is not unlike those men in white coats; he can't be trusted. He dares me to speak the words he long ago forced me to swallow. He requires of me an accusation, a confession, but he has not assailed me, he is not a priest, this is not an inquisition, I don't believe in God. I can no longer allow myself to think of Tadashi; he has gone the way of his words. Alone I must conjure another, finer image. I search for the face that has been more familiar to me than my own. Through the years it has remained a youthful face, that of the man I once loved. Why did Tadashi need to remind me, persist until now I cannot rest? I try to trace lines in the face of my beloved, but I see only my own face, the aged bones encased by skin too loose that Tadashi saw when he looked at me. My half-moon smile and lids creased shut are the only map I have. But a whisper of breath on my cheek, a secret shared in darkness is no longer enough. I must see his face, not as Tadashi saw mine; I must know his heart.

I dream of empty warehouses, blackened tunnels, cages with invisible bars, and awaken to the sight of Tomoe. Her tall body blocks the sunlight, her concern shadows my face. She says that I have been tugging at my tubes all night and that this type of behavior must stop.

"Don't you want to live?" she asks.

I can't understand what she means. She says, "I know this is not what you want.

"Grandma"—she calls me the name that has been mine since her children were born—"I want you to listen to me. Squeeze my hand if you are listening."

I cannot feel my own hands but something inside me

shifts and Tomoe takes hold. "I know that you must want to live or you would have let go long ago."

I look deeply into Tomoe's eyes and I imagine that I am in love with this woman. Not because she loves me—she doesn't—but because, unlike my mother, she has managed to express her hatred for me through acts of kindness.

For a second I imagine that I am a child again, but the truth is that I have no idea what I have become. I would like to believe that I have been reborn and that Tomoe is my mother. I would even settle for being the forty-nine-year-old woman I was thirteen days ago. I would like to be young and well and in love and not sick and dying in a bed that makes time go funny in my head. It's the drugs, I am told.

Percodan, Tegratol, Codeine, Valium. Now it's the death, my life banging against itself.

3
·
Tomoe

Summer comes late to San Francisco. Right around the time my girls go back to school in the fall, the fog lifts off the bay for a few days so that the ocean stretches out as far and long as the horizon will follow. It has a temperament as varied as any person I've come across. Sometimes green and so serene, other times blue and full of promise or black and just plain mean. I know color is only the reflection of sunlight and clouds, but I often wonder what's beneath all that water, swimming around, or swallowed by the tides.

On a morning as clear and bright as this one, my father went out on the ocean to fish. I was thirteen years old at the time, and what happened is not something I recall often or well. I only know that at this time of year, early in the morning before anyone else rises, the water catches on the window above the kitchen sink and I find myself thinking back.

He was a powerful man, my father, loved by those he favored and feared by those he hated. Both loved and feared by his wife and children. His boat washed up empty about a hundred miles down the coast from here, but to this day no one can be sure what happened to him. I don't remember Mama ever mourning him—maybe it was the shock of his sudden disappearance, or the fact that her life became easier once he was gone. Of course there was the problem of money. Mama must have worried where it would come from, how she would feed and clothe herself, my seven sisters, and me. Those difficulties would outlast my father, but without his moods to worry over, it was only a matter of work and making do. Mama used to tell me how sad it made her that she could not buy me a pair of patent leather shoes, and how every year she hoped to save enough money so that I could have a new dress for school. In Japan her family had money, so when she came to California she missed having nice things. But if I couldn't have nice shoes, or a new dress to wear, I hadn't had those things in the past, and so I could not have missed them. I didn't know about material things back then. I never knew exactly what I didn't have until I met Goro and became accustomed to the comforts his family takes for granted.

Now that my sisters and I are grown and married Mama lives alone. I try to call her each morning, but that isn't always possible. Just as I am dialing her number, Nomi comes into the kitchen rubbing her eyes. I can tell that she hasn't slept well, so I hang up the receiver and lift her onto my lap to eat her breakfast.

Nomi's scalp smells sweet and pure as the day she was born. She eats cornflakes in a soup of milk and the light from the window dazzles white from behind her black head.

"How is Grandma Rio today?" she asks.

On a day like today my father went out to sea never to return, so that on this day my mother lives alone. But how can a seven-year-old child be expected to understand? "Grandma Rio is going to be fine," I tell her. I do not say what I know, that my husband's mother lies in a hospital bed drifting over her own hazy sea.

"Did she ask about me?"

"I told her you miss her."

Nomi tells me she dreamt about her grandmother. "She was wearing a red dress and she looked very pretty, only she was fast asleep."

"When I met Grandma she was wearing a red dress."

Nomi shifts off my lap and takes her usual seat at the table. "When did you meet Grandma?"

I tell my youngest daughter about the night Goro brought me home to meet Rio and Tadashi. "Grandma came to the door with her hair all tied back in a white and red polka-dotted scarf. She wore a bright red dress with matching shoes and lipstick."

"Was she pretty?"

"She was beautiful." I was surprised at how beautiful she was. In all the months I'd dated Goro, he had never mentioned how beautiful his mother was.

Tadashi comes in from the yard. Like me he wakes up at the crack of dawn, only my domain is the house and his is the garden. He tends our front and backyards as expertly as he does his own route, which has been pretty much the same for twenty-five years. In twenty-five years I don't think he has ever missed a day's work, only lately he worries me. Since Rio's been gone his whole body seems weighted down. I could understand if it were after a day of planting, but even in the morning, after sleeping the night through, he still carries the weight with him. Most likely he can read my concern because his mouth curls into a funny smile when he sees me watching him. "How are you two this morning?"

"Mommy was telling me about the night she met you and Grandma Rio."

"That was—what—eleven years ago?"

"Mommy says Grandma was pretty."

"Grandma was beautiful." Tadashi plants himself in the middle of the room. For a second I'm afraid he's forgotten where he is, but that's the way he has always been at the sight of Rio or the mention of her name. Poor man, I think, still so in love with his once-beautiful wife.

"What else do you remember?" Nomi asks.

"We ate at this very table, only it was in Grandma Rio

and Grandpa Tadashi's old house." I run my hand over the nicks and scratches in the table's hardwood surface. "That night it was covered with a heavy white cloth and in the center was a glass vase full of pink peonies from Grandpa's garden."

"Ah, that's right, it was June then," says Tadashi.

"What did you eat, Grandpa?"

"We ate spaghetti," Tadashi says with a laugh. He is remembering now. I laugh too.

"Why is that so funny?" Nomi asks.

"I had never eaten anything like spaghetti."

"What do you mean?"

"Baachan, my mother, always made Japanese-styled vegetables, fish, and white rice for dinner."

"Spaghetti was your grandma's specialty."

My oldest, Melodie, enters the room and I pour some cereal for her. "What were you laughing about?" she asks.

"I was telling Nomi about the night I met Grandma Rio."

"What was she like?" Melodie asks.

"She was pretty," Nomi answers.

"You know who was even prettier?" Tadashi says.

"Who?" Nomi and Melodie chime in at once.

"Your mother. She was the prettiest thing Grandma and I had ever seen. And smart, too."

From the kitchen counter I watch my children's reaction to the compliment Tadashi has given me. Melodie squints at me over the top of her speckle-rim glasses and Nomi cocks her head. She is curious, but she doesn't quite understand. I wonder why they should look at me so strangely, but I am saved from having to think about it too carefully because Goro comes in ready for his breakfast and seconds later Granny starts in from above. I wonder if my mind is playing tricks on me or if the thump-thump of that woman's cane keeps getting louder. I can swear that one day soon she is going to fall through her floorboards and land smack-dab in the middle of our kitchen table, bed and all.

"Your cereal and coffee are on the counter," I tell my husband. "And you two had better go get dressed," I remind my daughters. "You're going to be late for school." As I climb the steps they crackle and creak beneath my feet.

Granny's room is directly above the kitchen so it too is flooded with light. But rather than pull the shades down at night, she sleeps wearing black eye-patches. As I make my way to her bed, I notice that she is still wearing them.

"Why don't you take those off now," I tell her.

"I don't need to see anything. It's just you, isn't it?"

I've learned to ignore Granny's caustic remarks. I am used to the ugly way her mouth turns down in a sneer, the black holes where her eyes should be. Still, some days I can barely stand to look at her.

"What's all that racket down there?" she demands.

"Everyone is eating breakfast. Same as usual," I tell her.

"Where's Rio?"

"She's still in the hospital."

"When are they letting her out?"

"We don't know yet."

"She doesn't expect me to pay for such a long stay, does she? You'd better tell them to let her out."

"I'll get you some breakfast."

"I'm not hungry."

"What do you want then?"

"Where's Rio?"

"She's in the hospital."

"When are they letting her out?"

"We don't know yet."

"She's been there a long time now." Granny pauses, and the curve of her mouth relaxes. I wipe a drop of spittle from her chin.

"You must miss her."

"Where has she been?"

I will never understand how Granny's mind works—the way it clicks on and off at its leisure while her daughter lies half-dead in a hospital bed after trying to take her own life. If Reiko were my mother I'd set her straight right away. But Reiko and Rio are Goro's grandmother and mother, not mine, and I have two daughters of my own to worry about. "I have to take the girls to school now. Are you sure you don't want breakfast?"

"When can I go home?" she calls after me as I walk away.

"I want to go with you to the hospital to visit Grandma Rio." Nomi's eyes meet mine as I back the car out of the garage.

After righting myself in the seat I steer straight ahead. "Hospitals are not for children," I tell her.

"I've been to the hospital," Melodie says, "the time I hurt my finger." From the rearview mirror I can see how Melodie holds her finger up to the light to check for scarring. Then she jabs Nomi in the ribs. "You wouldn't like it there."

I have reminded my girls over and over to stay seated in the back while I am driving, but Nomi stands up on the floor mat and wraps her arms around my neck. "I still want to go with you," she whispers in my ear.

I steer the car past rows of houses, colorful boxes stacked up and down the hills, one after another, each one holding another family, each family with its own problems. From the outside all the houses look the same, only on the inside they are as different as can be. I want to explain this to Nomi. I want both my daughters to find security in the way things appear; to know that people who travel too deeply within face danger. While they are young, I want them to know safety. "Sit back," I tell my youngest. "You're going to cause an accident."

"Will Grandma Rio die?" Nomi resumes her position next to Melodie.

"She might." I have answered this question a hundred times, but Nomi is too young to understand.

"Will you die?" Nomi asks.

"We will all die someday."

"Will you die soon?" Melodie asks.

"You never know," I tell her. "But I don't think so."

Normally it takes me seventeen minutes to drive my daughters to school and back again, but these last two weeks my morning routine has been disrupted by trips to the hospital. Each morning after dropping Melodie and Nomi at the front gate, I have to remind myself about Grandma, and turn off in the opposite direction of home. It's hard to believe this has been going on for thirteen days now. Thirteen long days, yet not even two weeks ago I was the one who discovered her.

I can't help but think what would have happened had my morning gone differently that day. It was Friday, I know because after the girls went to school I washed and changed the sheets. At about eleven, when I went up to do Granny's, she said she wanted a grilled cheese sandwich, so I made one for her lunch, but when I brought it upstairs and found her sleeping I decided to take it down to Rio, since she'd been too depressed lately to cook for herself.

It was dark downstairs and the bedroom door was opened slightly, which is unusual for Grandma. Then I heard the strangest moaning. It was barely audible, but it reminded me of the sound the neighbor's cat used to make when she went into heat. Summers when I was growing up that cat used to keep me awake all night. I thought at first that Grandma's radio was on. When she can't sleep she'll play the news channel for days at a time, but when I listened carefully I knew I wasn't hearing the radio. I kept thinking how being a mother teaches you to stand so quietly outside a door, listening for noise at night when your children are supposed to be asleep, and that's probably why I managed to stay put long enough for my eyes to adjust to the darkness, and then I saw her. She was spread out all perfect on her bed sheet, her arms folded neatly over her chest, and a peaceful, half smile I'd never seen before seemed to light up her face. "Grandma," I called to her from the doorway. When she didn't respond I dropped the tray I'd been holding and ran to her bedside. "Grandma, wake up!" I shouted in her ear and shook her, and when that didn't work I phoned the operator right away and asked for an ambulance to be sent. Then my fingers dialed the church. "Bay Community Church, good morning," Goro's secretary, Chieko, picked up.

"This is Tomoe." I could hear my own voice and I

checked it for strain. Chieko is so nosy; she mustn't suspect a problem. "I need to speak with Goro, is he there?"

Chieko told me to hold the line, she mustn't suspect, and during the silence, while I stood vigil over his mother, a line of scripture repeated itself in my head: *And we know that all things work together for the good of those who love God, and those who are called according to his purpose.* Clearly this situation did not apply. But what was taking Goro so long? I imagined him leafing through the Bible for some applicable passage of scripture to use in Sunday's sermon, how he hates to be disturbed when he's thinking, until my own thoughts began to scare me. By the time he came on the line I was ready to hang up, but I told him as best I could how I found Grandma and that I'd already called an ambulance.

"Is she conscious?" The fear in his voice reassured me.

I looked at her lying there, and her expression was so serene that I lowered my voice. "No," I whispered, "not at all."

"Slap her cheek."

"What?" I raised my free hand to shield the mouthpiece.

"Slap her," he said patiently, "to try to get a response."

In that instant I could feel my own body towering over her. Then I bent down and slapped her, harder than I should have because my fingertips went numb.

"Tomoe." I could hear Goro calling me back. "Please answer me, dear."

"Yes." I felt an urge to apologize. "Nothing."

"Okay." Goro drew a deep breath. "Is she alive, Tomoe?"

"Yes." I could not be sure, but something in me sensed that the life had not gone out of her.

There was a silence, and then Goro's voice clicked in again. "Can you get her out of bed?"

"Yes."

"Stand her up then and walk with her. Walk her around the room as best you can. Do you understand?"

"Yes."

"Tell the ambulance driver to take her to Hillview Hospital and I'll meet her there. I'm going to hang up now."

I am a strong woman. I can carry my daughters one in each arm if I have to, but moving Grandma was no easy task. She may look thin, but she's built solid inside.

That day, with the life flowing thick through me, I wasn't scared to hold Rio in my arms; I even felt reassured by the density of her weight. But now that my own life has been upset, I must admit to myself that part of me regrets having found her at all. I can feel good about doing what needed to be done, but almost two weeks have gone by now. The doctors have pumped her stomach and tested her blood and she is going to live. That's why when I exchange pleasantries with the receptionist at the front desk, what I'm really feeling is how tired I'm getting of all this.

Mama taught me to respect life; that Rio tried to take her own life shows disrespect for her family. If she ever stopped to consider her son and grandchildren, what such behavior would do to them, let alone what it's now doing to me, none of this would be happening. But Rio is selfish, and so it's hard to know what she could have been thinking that morning, or what she's thinking now.

This morning for the first time Grandma's eyes are open, and I can tell she knows I'm here. I should say something to her because for two weeks now I have been talking to her in my head, but suddenly I have no words. Her brows curve in thin, delicate lines and beneath them her eyes are sunken and not seeing. There is sadness in her face, and because I can't imagine what would make a person so sad, I am sad for her. Even in this despondent state she is beautiful, and I am both repelled and seduced by what I cannot understand.

When I return home I am surprised to find Tadashi still seated at the kitchen table. "I noticed the roses out front are still blooming," I say, because I don't want him to think I think badly of him for getting off to a late start. "You've done such a nice job with them this year."

"It's nothing," he says. "Did you stop by to see Grandma on your way home?"

"Yes."

"How did she seem?"

"About the same," I tell him. "How are you?"

"About the same."

"Granny didn't make a fuss while I was away, did she?"

"No."

Tadashi props his elbows on the table and rubs his forehead with both hands, letting me know it's okay to say something. "This must be a very hard time for you." I offer him my sympathy.

"I'll be all right," he says. "I meant what I said this morning, Tomoe. You were the most beautiful woman Grandma and I had ever seen. Goro is a lucky man."

"Damned lucky!" I use Tadashi's expression in an attempt to cheer him up. I tell him that in the eleven years I've known him, I still can't get over how the most respectful, proudest man I've ever met is always saying *damned lucky, damned good.*

Tadashi raps his palms on the table and laughs. "Hot damn."

I know he meant to flatter me when he said that Goro is lucky, but I respond by joking with him because I can't tell him what I'd like to say. Even though I know I have been a good wife to my husband, he deserves far more credit than me. He isn't Goro's natural father, but he has sacrificed for Goro more than most fathers are willing to do for their own. Looking across the table at a man who has aged by years in the last couple of weeks, I think it's a crime that his family hasn't treated him better. I can't do anything about Rio, but I try to tell Goro that his attitude toward Tadashi isn't right. I tell him his problem is that he's spoiled, but he ignores me. You can't tell people things they don't want to hear, it just doesn't work. I'm thinking exactly that when I realize that the knocking from above has started in again and that Tadashi has been trying to get my attention. "Should I go up?" he asks.

"No, she can wait a few minutes."

"You seem a little tired, maybe you should try not to do too much today."

I tell Tadashi that I'm not tired, but he doesn't pay any attention. He tells me he's finished with his gardening route for the morning, so he can take care of Granny.

"I'm fine," I try to reassure him. "Besides, I don't need too much time to myself. You know me."

"I know you," he says, "that's the trouble."

"There's no trouble," I say.

Then he becomes thoughtful. "Everyone should have something they do just for themselves. Rio didn't, you know."

I am not used to hearing Tadashi speak so directly, and yet I don't understand what he's talking about. I try to hear him, but my eyes turn instinctively to the ceiling where the knocking persists. "I'd better go see to Granny now," I tell him.

Then, as if he's read my mind, he says, "Granny isn't going anywhere. Nomi and Melodie can take care of her and themselves in the afternoons, and I think Goro would agree with me."

"What would I do?" I wonder aloud. Unlike my husband I didn't have the opportunity to go to college. I barely finished high school.

"What would you like to do?"

"I'd have to think about it," I tell him, and quickly now I disappear up the stairs before he can stop me.

Do something for yourself. What would you like to do? I can't help but repeat Tadashi's words while I change Granny's soiled sheets. It figures that on this day their acrid odor gives me a headache, and the garbage bag lets loose all over my just-mopped kitchen floor. I never get headaches, I hate messes. I should know by now that things like this will happen, but when a can of tuna fish clanks to the floor I am tempted to kick it into a corner. *Forget it,* I tell myself as I wipe away the fishy smell. Standing over the sink washing a head of lettuce for Granny's lunch I try to concentrate on the cool water trickling between my fingers. I take my time with each leaf, stopping every few minutes to look out the window. But instead of good thoughts, my mind conjures morbid images of Granny. I see her bloated body floating on the edge of the shoreline, charred by overexposure to the sun. Then the tap water becomes gritty and the lettuce turns slimy to the touch. I feel as though I'm holding on to a rootless bed of sea kelp—that's when I know I'm not thinking straight. I know Tadashi did not mean to criticize the way I live, but no one has ever suggested to me that I do something on my own, or asked me what I'd like for myself. He should not have said what he said because once you speak you can't take it back.

His words force me to imagine what my life will be like when my children are grown and gone. They will have their own lives one day. They will marry and have children, and they will grow further and further away until one day I may not even recognize them as my own. And a woman cannot count on her husband. When I suggest to Goro that he might help out with dinner he says I should hire a maid. "We can afford one," he says. He looks at me as if he thinks I'm stupid; he doesn't see that he has missed the point altogether.

The point is that I was raised to believe that doing something for myself means caring for others and Goro grew up believing that caring for himself is enough. He comes home at the end of the day, kisses me on the cheek, and then disappears into his study. Alone late at night, I often wonder what he could possibly be doing in there. A man does find satisfaction, as Goro claims, in books. But that is not what I mean to say. The point is that Goro is never around to begin with, my girls will have their own homes one day, and where will that leave me? I have to laugh when I think of devoting the rest of my life to my husband's grandmother. Being so wicked she will no doubt outlive us all. And who knows whether Rio will survive, or if she does what she will need when she recovers. One thing I do know: Whatever happens, Tadashi can take care of himself.

If I could do anything I wanted, I know what I would do. I remember walking to school one day and finding an old photograph of a couple sunbathing on a tropical beach. I kept it under my pillow at night and carried it in my pocket during the day because I wanted to believe that I existed on the same planet as that beautiful landscape, those beautiful people. Now the air off the shore is fragrant and warm. From my kitchen window the world opens up into an expanse of sky and sea that lets me know I could be almost anywhere.

I remember my father, how nothing ever slipped by his careful eye. It is the same with Tadashi; though he rarely voices opinions about members of our household, no one should be fooled by his calm. Most likely Tadashi has said what he needed to say to me because he sees in me a daughter. If so, that is fine with me. I am not ashamed to say that I love him more than I ever loved my own father.

I rush my daughters through dinner, hurry them through their baths and tuck them into bed even though I know they will not sleep for at least another hour. If they weren't so young I'd talk with them first, but I have waited all day to be able to call Mama.

"Hello, Mama," I say excitedly in Japanese.

"Patti-chan?" She mistakes me for my sister.

"No, it's Tomoe."

"Ah, Tomoe. How are you?"

"Just fine. How is work?"

"Not too bad lately." She isn't one to complain, but I can hear the strain in her voice.

"You mustn't work too hard." My mother is past the age of retirement, but she's worked every day for as long as I can remember. If she had a son, she could go and live with him. I wish she could live with me, but my life is already too full with Granny, and now Grandma.

"Don't worry about me."

"I'm sorry I haven't called for a few days." I know she's lonely, all by herself now that her children all have lives of their own. Even my youngest sister, Patti, is married now.

"I'll try to come visit this weekend."

"That sounds good. Patti said she'll try to make it down too. How is Rio-san?"

"She's doing better." It's a necessary lie. Mama lives in Oakland, only a half hour's drive from here, but there's no denying the bridge that must be crossed. I want to tell Mama what Tadashi has said. There is so much of the world to be traveled, and wouldn't it be nice if I could send her to Japan one day. Poor thing hasn't seen her family in over forty years!

I know what I want to do now, but I can't make promises to other people yet, especially to Mama. Besides, another day's energy has slipped past us both. At the other end of the house I can hear my daughters sharing their secrets across the thin wall that joins their rooms. Mama's tired voice barely touches my ear, but their chatter rings with life.

Kindling and
Bedflame

4

.

N o m i

You begin as a sudden conception of myself, except older, and everything I want I already have. My hips aren't narrow and bony anymore—they curve like the bottom of a summer squash, and balance perfectly beneath my long waist because I've grown tall, taller even than my mother, and my breasts are heavy enough so that I can feel them rising and falling just above my ribcage when I breathe. On a gray day in the middle of spring I lie on the grass in the middle of the garden Grandpa Tadashi keeps, imagining I live in some foreign city, alone, with a man who is older than me, and handsome, and he knows things about me without having to ask.

I started high school this year and I should be there right now, but who cares? I go off with Melodie in the morning, before my mother and father leave the house, but by noon I'm home again, in the backyard because that is the place I like to come. It's nice to lie here, where there are things that can be counted on. Like the bonsai, which are always the same size. Their purple and white flowers blossom in spring as if by faith. Towering over me a row of hedges has been carefully pruned by Grandpa Tadashi to resemble lanky giraffes and rabid, prehistoric dogs. I used to watch while Grandpa stood on a ladder trimming a giraffe's neck, a dog's ear. When I asked him once why he didn't just let them grow wild, he said he had to clip them to protect the house from termites. But I didn't hear termites. I saw long necks and eyes and teeth.

Today, for a change, I am not alone. I have brought my friend Eric with me through the gate and into the backyard. He lies on top of me and I watch the sky, pale behind his shiny black eyes. Then we lock our legs together and roll over and I have to laugh at the way blades of grass stick straight out between strands of his thick black hair. Pretty soon our sweat smells like the browns and greens of dirt and grass.

I am not exactly sure why I have invited Eric home with me, except that I'm glad he is here. Looking at the windows that lead into the house from the outside, I know that Granny lies in her bed just beyond the glass on the top floor, and that Grandma can be found down the stairs that lead to the lower patio. They are so close, but the windows keep them away. Grandma Rio can't know I'm out here with Eric because she can't see well enough, and Granny Reiko might know, but won't be believed. This means that I am safe; my parents are at work, there is no Granny no Grandma no school.

Eric withdraws his tongue from my mouth. "Are you sure this is okay, Nomi?" he whispers.

"Are you kidding?" I lick his ear. "This is great."

I am liking Eric because my mind can travel anywhere when I am with him and he does not have to know. He isn't me, does not even know who I am.

And so you begin with Eric. At first you are Eric. You are the one so close to me who is not me. You begin as the thing I have hoped for, to travel outside myself and far away.

When Eric and I stand side by side, our arms dangling in a V, our faces crowning the fence, the bay, which is barely visible beneath thick cloud cover, does not look the same. "Just think, there are things *living* in all that water," Eric says.

"Sharks," I say.

"Nah," he says, "beautiful fish—whole schools of them —and the farther out you go the better they get."

"Hmmm," I say, "I'm not really into fish."

"You're kidding," he says. "I'm going to go to college in Hawaii when we graduate. They have fish there that would blow you away."

"You blow me away," I tell him.

I daydream about Eric. I walk gracefully from the kitchen down the hall to my bedroom, believing he is just beyond my eyeline, silently approving of the way I walk, the way my chin tilts slightly up, the black hair that fans out behind me.

"Nomi's become such an oshare-san." I hear my mother whisper *primadonna*. She is talking to Grandma Rio in the other room, but her voice carries to my room. She wants me to hear.

"Such a pretty head of hair." Grandma does not whisper. Her comment is meant for me.

"It should be pretty," my mother whispers again, "for all the conditioning and blow-drying that goes on around here."

I roll my eyes, wishing my mother would choke.

"Say, Rio"—wishing does me no good—"when I brought Granny her dinner tonight she said that she saw Nomi in the backyard in the middle of the day. You didn't see her, did you?"

"Let's see."

I can't see Grandma, but I imagine the way she looks when she's deep in thought, her nose and eyebrows twisted up. "She'd be at school then, wouldn't she?"

"I certainly hope so." My mother practically screams this, a threat.

I sit in front of my dresser mirror mimicking my mother. Her mouth is full, like mine, and I flatten my lips into a perfect, nasty sneer. So what if I'm not at school during the day? I finger the place on the mirror where my lips reflect back, imperfectly. The image I touch is hard, flat, impenetrable, but inside I am mush. I am miserable and I don't even know why, except that in the kitchen my mother sits wondering what exactly she can think to do to make me feel worse. I try to imagine my life without her. What if she were to go to work one morning and not come home? But that will never happen. If anyone is going to disappear it is going to be me. I am thinking this, wondering where I might go, when my eyes return to the face staring back at me. It isn't bad. It might even be pretty, but above my eyes I am all eyebrows. I have never noticed this before, the way my eyebrows practically connect in the middle into one straight line like a thick black cloud hanging over my face.

Fortunately I've seen my mother tweeze her brows enough times to know what to do. I am left-handed so I begin with the left side, pulling the skin on my forehead up with my right hand, and slowly, with my left hand, removing the hairs one by one. Each time I pull back on the tweezers my eyes burn and tear until I can barely see.

In the other room, my mother is still talking. I can hear bits and pieces of what she is saying, and I hate myself for listening. What she suspects I've been doing lately has led, as it usually does, into everything she dislikes about me. ". . . gained ten pounds in the last year." ". . . will never get into a good college at this rate. WHY IS SHE SO BOY CRAZY ALL OF A SUDDEN?"

The fact is, I'm not crazy at all. My mother is the one who's so crazy, and listening to her makes me wish I were with Eric. He says he's going to go to Hawaii for college.

He will live among schools of fish, a whole ocean full, and the farther out you go the better they get. *You are out of here.* My breath fogs the mirror, and I watch a tear drip down my cheek. I may not yet be an adult, but I am old enough to know I'm not a child anymore either, and I hate being locked inside this house like some convict.

I want to run away, and I wish I could think where to go. I am so drowsy I could fall back on my bed and sleep forever, but every time my eye catches my reflection in the mirror I have to laugh because my head looks so lopsided. Instead of pulling the hairs patiently, one by one, I yank whole clumps out of the right side. The pain is intense for a second, but then it's gone. The only problem is that it's hard to match the right side to the left. I pluck a few more hairs from the left, then the right, until I barely have anything left up there. Strawberry patches dot the places where hairs used to be, and when I press a tissue to my forehead it comes away bloody.

I consider not leaving my room ever again, but in the morning my father taps me on the shoulder to wake me up for school. "Get up, baby," he says. 'Your mother's been calling you and you're going to be late."

"Daddy?" I say. I am still dreaming, and in my dream I have forgotten how mad I am at everyone. But as his face comes into focus I remember my eyebrows and pull the sheet up over my head.

"Stop playing around," he says. "Now what's the matter?"

"Nothing." I pull the sheet down again and run my fingers through my hair to brush it back. "Do you notice anything different about me?" I lift my chin and force a big smile.

"Did you get a new nightgown?"

"No."

"What is it, then?" He is impatient.

"Nothing."

When he goes, I look in the mirror wondering how it could be possible that he didn't notice.

Melodie is in the bathroom, and I pull my hair back so she can see, but she just shrugs her shoulders. "They'll grow back," she mumbles with a mouth full of toothpaste.

Looking in my mirror by daylight, I reassess the damage. Maybe it is not so great. I can always pencil in the holes, the way Grandma Rio does hers. Then, at breakfast, my mother reaches across the table and pulls the hair away from my forehead. "What have you done?"

"Honestly," she shakes her head, "they were so pretty the way they were."

"Well, thanks a lot," I say. Didn't she know how painful it was to remove all those hairs? If she's so observant, couldn't she see the pools of blood the tweezers left behind?

Grandma Rio waits for me every afternoon, but it has been days since I've gone downstairs to visit her. It's like my mother says, How can a person sleep all day? She never *does* anything. But that's why I try so hard to make her happy. When I was younger, I took piano lessons for three years just because I knew she liked to hear me play. I hated every minute of practicing and my mother knew it. She said, "If you want to play that's one thing, but you don't seem to enjoy it and I drive you back and forth twice a week and pay seven dollars a lesson. Think about it."

I thought about it, but I couldn't quit. My teacher was a fat old lady with a funny accent. *You're sooo talented, Nomi. Why not practice a little more? Even ten minutes a day is better than nutting, no?* I'd leave her house every week vowing to practice more, try harder. Then my mother would say, "What are you doing watching TV, talking on the phone, PRACTICE YOUR PIANO." And my grandmother downstairs waiting every second for something beautiful to pop out of my fingertips. Alone in the living room, I'd pound through my scales as fast as I could, and when I made a mistake I'd bang the keys with my fists. Then I'd play my Tarantellas, Minuets, Sonatinas, without looking at the scores, without counting, totally numb. For my ninth birthday Grandma bought me a metronome, one of those old-fashioned wooden ones with a needle that swings back and forth, *tick, tick, tick,* until one day I tore the needle from its hinges and scratched it across the mahogany surface of the piano, and my mother must have told my grandmother because when I visited her she said, "You know, Nomi, you don't have to play if you don't enjoy it."

It was my teacher who finally made me quit. She said she didn't want to waste her *talons* anymore on someone who wasn't interested. Still, I must be the biggest fool of all because when I finally gather myself up to go downstairs, I see Grandma lying there, so small and motionless in the middle of her bed, and I tell her over and over how much I've missed her. I kiss her cheek to show her I mean it. *I will always protect you, always.* So many layers of bedding practically swallow her up, but I tuck the sheets beneath the mattress and give her pillows a few slaps. *You are safe now. I will never let anything bad happen to you again.*

Bits of dust spin through the light and Grandma sits up. "It's not you," I confide as the dust settles, but it is her, and heat begins building behind my eyeballs. Why do I have to be the one to come downstairs and visit? I hate sitting here in this dark room with its funny smells and my grandmother whose life seems to depend on me alone. I have a sudden urge to run, but I don't. I look down at my hands in my lap. "I'm sorry I haven't been downstairs to visit in so long."

"Don't be sorry." She laughs because she's so happy to see me again. "Now tell me, what's wrong?"

I have to think for a minute because I don't know what's wrong anymore. *She's so happy to see me again.* "I want to go away," I tell her, "but where? Where would you go if you could go anywhere?"

"Anywhere on this earth?"

"Yes, of course. Where else would I mean?"

"Well, then," Grandma squints and purses her lips, "it would have to be somewhere I haven't been. Somewhere familiar but far away."

My eyes travel to the colorful silkscreen above her bed where a familiar woman stands in a blue chrysanthemum-patterned kimono. Her expression is almost comical —nose turned up and eyes crossed in disgust. But something is wrong. The obi around her waist is gone, leaving only a thin string to hold so many chrysanthemums in place, and a pointy breast sticks out where the kimono hangs open in front. Why have I never noticed this before?

"Is that you?" I point at the woman on the wall.

Grandma turns her head to see what I'm looking at. Then she begins to laugh. "No. She's probably a geisha."

"You're kidding," I say. "You mean a prostitute?"

"Geisha aren't prostitutes," Grandma says. "They are well trained in traditional Japanese arts, and they can sing and dance, too."

"Hmmmm," I say. "I wonder what happened to her."

"I wonder too."

"Why do you have her hanging over your bed?" I ask, because now that I've noticed the painting I can't stop looking at her.

"I don't know, I guess I've always liked her." Grandma smiles. "You're not thinking of going off to Japan and becoming a geisha, are you?"

"No," I giggle, "I'm not the geisha type."

"Well, that's a relief," she says.

But it isn't long before the blue chrysanthemum woman starts appearing everywhere. In a dream I am running down an alley to escape gunfire and she pulls me behind a wall and hides me under the deep folds of her kimono. At school she is the tall girl who shows me how to tie my hair in a knot on my head using a pencil to hold it in place, and on my way home she is the bush of gardenias burning white against the afternoon sky.

Then one night I have this dream: I am in an outdoor restaurant, close to water because the sound of it floods my ears, and I am being waited on by a stranger. I can't see his face, only his arms, a man's arms with dark hair on the fingers serving me the most delicious food imaginable. Tempura with batter so light it disappears on my tongue and somen noodles, my favorite, which I can't stop eating. The raw tuna is the faintest shade of pink, and I know that when it is gone I will know who this man is, so I eat quickly, vigorously, until his arms disappear and suddenly the woman in the blue chrysanthemum kimono is waving her billowy silk sleeves for me to follow. We agree to meet in Japan, but when I wake up I can't be sure if I have gone and come back or not left yet. I am alone in my bed, exhausted; certain my dream is real, I say to myself: "I'll meet you in Japan, then."

I don't believe in God, but I think that he has spoken to me in my own voice, maybe in the same way my

mother says God spoke to my father last week and told
him to leave the church. I don't know if my father will
listen to God, or, if he does, what he is supposed to do,
but I wake up knowing I must go to Japan. As the days
unfold I know I have never wanted anything more desper-
ately in my life.

I will work hard to get to Japan, and I spend the summer
scooping ice cream to prove to my mother that this is
true. I earn $2.13 an hour, which, I know, does not
amount to much, but I open a savings account with my
first week's wages because this is the way to show how
serious I am. I might never get to Japan with the $500 I
can save by the end of summer, but the strength I develop
from scooping ice cream burns my left wrist and makes me
believe I cannot be stopped. From the start Japan and you
are linked into one: Japan is the dream that keeps me
sticking my head into the ice cream case, and every time I
come up holding another round scoop you are the promise of life beyond my grandmother, my mother, my father,
my sister Melodie, and everyone else I know.

I see Eric when he stops by for a cone, nights after
closing and on whichever day of the week I have off. On a
Sunday in July he takes me to the Aquarium, where there
must be a million different species of fish. I have come
here before, with my parents as a child and many more
times growing up, but on this day standing in the dark in

front of a tank full of anglers, I think I have never seen anything so beautiful. Dorsal fins drape over their mouths like veils to lure the unsuspecting prey. Mesmerized by the swooping motion that is both seamless and utterly calculated, I kiss Eric's shoulder to let him know I see what he sees. He turns to me proud, and with an open mouth displays his large white teeth. "I love you," he says.

"What?" I need to hear it again.

"I love you."

I believe, at that moment, with the anglers swimming circles around me in the dark, that life cannot get any better. I have a boyfriend who says he loves me until I am bursting from so much love, and in less than a year I will leave for Japan.

You are some flaw in my logic that allows me to mistake a sudden appreciation of fish for love, and love for a desire to be someplace far away. Still, do not underestimate longing. As swiftly as love struck I am drowning. Certain I cannot tolerate another minute in the darkened auditorium, I grab Eric's hand and pull him toward the nearest exit. In the daylight of Golden Gate Park I discover a quiet place, not far from the Arboretum, where trees grow restlessly into the sky. My heart still rushes, but the landscape here is not tame and familiar like Grandpa Tadashi's garden and I can no longer be sure whether what I feel is panic or excitement. Maybe for that reason I let Eric's tongue explore my neck with my eyes wide open. In a place where neither gates nor walls nor windows conceal us, I feel the crotch of his pants grow stiff between my legs, and I slide shamelessly to the ground.

"Can we get arrested for this?" Eric wants to know.

"Not if we're quiet." I pull him down on top of me. I want quiet, and to feel the whole of his weight pinning my back to the earth, and I pray he will not stop.

5

·

R i o

It begins above my head. A door creaking open, then shut, then Nomi's footsteps, slower than usual. I feel the hinges like my joints: a storm is coming.

I married young, and not for love. I was fifteen when I met my first husband. Sadamichi was a customer at my mother's barbershop, a transient on his way from San Francisco to Los Angeles, and our introduction came in the form of my washing his scalp.

I still remember the first words he spoke to me as I bent over the washbasin. "Scrub harder, Rio." My mother must have told him my name. I remember the Liberty dollar he slipped down the bodice of my dress, how heavy and solid it felt. I can still feel his eyes watching me as I shimmied to get the cold metal away from my skin, hear him laughing himself into a fit as I chased the coin across the smooth linoleum floor.

When I reached out my arm to hand it back to him, he refused. "A tip," he called it.

I should have given his money back without hesitation. No good that he was, I should have thrown it at him. But instead I held that Liberty dollar palm up to the light and let it warm there.

Though she had money to spare, my mother never offered to pay me for my labor, and so it never occurred to me that money was a thing I could have. Nor did I see how anyone could be interested in me, a fifteen-year-old who used belts and safety pins to reshape her mother's dresses that had long since gone out of style.

At fifteen, my days were spent mixing up harsh shampoos, but even sudsy water was not enough to cleanse the odor of dirty scalps from my hands. At night my shoulders ached and I imagined that my spine had become permanently hunched from bending over the washbasin.

I knew my real deformities were not the kind that showed in the mirror, still I did not know what a girl who worked in her mother's barbershop could have to offer a man. Slowly I let my fingers curl around the Liberty dollar that Sadamichi offered me, but that day I did not accept it. Not because I didn't want to, but because I did not believe in myself. And so when Sadamichi asked me days later to marry him, I accepted his proposal as if I'd been waiting for it my whole life.

■ ■ ■

"You are lucky," I tell Nomi when she brings her report card downstairs for me to examine. "With your brain you can do anything you want with your life." *When I was your age, I was married with Goro on the way.*

"I know," she says, "but school is just a matter of learning what's expected of you."

She is very self-assured for a fifteen-year-old. "Some day soon you might find a subject that challenges you, then you will come to think differently."

"I didn't even attend half of my geometry classes." *She is not at the age yet where she can understand.* "I made friends with the teacher's aide, who told me when to show up for the tests, and the teacher is so blind and forgetful that he didn't even know the difference. Can you believe that?"

"It is hard to believe."

"Do you want to know what his name is?"

"Yes," I laugh, "tell me."

"His name is Eric." She smiles, not at me but at some point inside my head. *She is looking inside my head, prying through brain and bilge.*

"What do your mother and father think about Eric?"

Nomi rolls her eyes, then she squeezes my hand. "I would never tell them, just you. You know why?"

"Why?" My mouth is dry. *I do not want to know.*

"Because I am just like you."

"Oh, no." I shake my head. "Our hearts are the same, but nothing else."

"What else matters?"

"You are so young," I tell her, "and maybe you are right."

Nomi has a mother and father who love her. She does not need to understand that hearts are only muscles, that they can only beat in time.

The morning I left San Francisco, I carried my bags down the steps that lead away from my mother's house on tiptoe with my heart pounding in my ears. It was summer, and my truest thoughts as I waited on the curb were as hidden to me as whatever lay beneath the morning fog. I did not wonder what would happen if Sadamichi could not stay with me, or, worse yet, if I could not stay with him. I concentrated on nothing more tangible than how good it felt to be leaving my mother, never to smell the rank odor of old men, never to have to scrape the dirt from their heads out from under my nails. Never again in my life.

I was squinting to see the bay through the fog when Sadamichi's jalopy began climbing the hill. It was a terrible green car, shaped like a coffin on wheels. When it overheated passing through the grapevine, Sadamichi climbed on top of the roof and began picking through my belongings.

"You won't need a coat in Los Angeles."

I watched through the rearview mirror; I could not move. In the blink of an eye, Sadamichi must have thought he could discard the past that had bound me to my mother, and that day I saw everything I owned drop to the dirt. I knew I should have felt lighter, freer, but as the car rolled away a heaviness settled in my heart that I could not have anticipated. I couldn't speak. What was there to say? *Los Angeles* had been repeating in my head for days, though I no longer knew what it meant. I had not been gone for more than a few hours when I found myself longing to return home.

Ten years ago I wished for death until my life hovered like a seagull before my eyes, and now I am growing old only to find that time moves backwards. It's uncanny: like waking from a dream I've had more than once, the anticipation once quenched burning strong again.

Not long after my arrival home from Hillview, my granddaughters traipsed down the stairs together to visit me. Being a year older, Melodie led the way, examining the contents on my dresser, casting her gaze in my direction, but always stopping short of getting a good look at me. Maybe she feared I would look different. Maybe to her I did. She held on tightly to her younger sister's hand, and obediently Nomi hid behind her shoulder.

"Is that you back there, Nomi?" I asked at last.

Nomi brushed past Melodie and tiptoed to my bedside. Inches away from my face she bent over and pressed her nose so close to my scalp that I could hear the faint rush of her breathing, taste her sweet smell. Then a bright smile appeared on her face and she wrapped her skinny arms around my shoulders.

"Come here, Melodie," I called past Nomi's swell of hair. I could see Melodie standing anxiously at the foot of my bed. "Come give Grandma a hug."

Melodie did not budge. She wanted no part of me or my hugs, that afternoon or in the days to come. Most likely she was old enough even back then to have been told how close to death I had come and how precariously I still lingered. I would like to believe that Nomi understood too, but that she also recognized that death could never change how we felt about each other. But Nomi no longer visits me every day. I know what this means; still I wait, hoping against the clearest of evidence. I wait and I try to remember every detail of our last conversation. *When I was your age, I was married with a child on the way. I knew love, and yes, hate.* If she returns, I promise never to trouble her again with my past. Patiently, I wait, and when Tadashi comes home at the end of the day, I hide my troubles from him.

Then come the phone calls. Ringing above my bed and secrets whispered late into the night. Nomi's visits stop, making me wonder whether I was ever more than a burden to her, a distraction in her day. I'd like to believe that it's different between her and me. I need to believe in the substance that binds two lives, something as fluid as water, like the love I once had, and as solid as the flesh that connects me to my mother, me to Nomi. That feeling has always run strong through me and I must not doubt. But maybe it is only habit that brings Nomi to me. And if this is so, then my tie to life itself is as tenuous as it's always been. But just when I've given up hope, Nomi reappears as if she'd never gone.

"You must eat more," I tell her, because I notice that her cheeks have lost their fleshiness and that her demeanor is no longer gay or carefree. The youthful odor of sweat and play is now masked by a sweet perfume, and I don't say anything but I wonder why she tweezed away her eyebrows that were once so full and expressive. Then the arguments come—Goro, Tomoe, even Melodie becomes involved. I cannot make out what they say to one another, only anger, then silence. Then the footsteps again; they lead away in slow, heavy movement.

Having left Sadamichi and returned home expecting the worst, I could not have guessed that I would be greeted at the door as if I'd never gone away. "Rio, come in," my mother raised her fingers to her powdery white cheek, "and who is this?"

"His name is Goro, Mother."

"Well then, Rio, Goro," she led me into the living room, ignoring her new grandson (whom I carried like a flag), gesturing as she walked, "I want you to meet D."

In the living room a tallish Caucasian man occupied the chair that my mother had long ago called my father's, and as it turned out D. was my mother's third husband. Before that afternoon I hadn't known his name, but I remembered him vaguely as a customer, someone my mother had once spoken of as the "kanemochi banker," the "hakujin" who liked "nice Japanese ladies." Once again I was the outsider. After dinner it was D. who brought out tea, and my mother winked at me as if to say, See how well my life goes on without you. If you thought I missed you, now you know that you are as replaceable as the next person. And that was what seemed curious: not that D. seemed charmed by everything she did and said, but of all the men who had ingratiated themselves before her, why had she chosen him?

Before Goro's eyes my mother and her house were all delightfully new: his excitement revealed a world hidden to me. As I carried him from room to room he held his hands out wanting to touch everything—the leather encasing my great-grandfather's ceremonial sword, an antique Japanese doll that belonged to my grandmother, the piano I was taught as a child never to touch, even the urn containing my grandfather's ashes which my mother kept so morbidly beside the fireplace. I expected him to be fussy in a new place, around two new people, but when I finally put him down, he crawled straight to the couch where my mother and D. sat and used his eager fists to climb between them. What gall young children have!

I would have tried to stop him, but D. encouraged his curiosity. One day, a few weeks after I'd moved in, I was folding up a stack of diapers and singing to Goro; I'd wanted to get him to sleep so that I could be on time at my waitressing shift when D. appeared with my grandfather's mandolin and began to strum an old Japanese children's song. *Where does spring come from? I wonder where it comes from. It comes from the mountains, it comes from the ocean. That must be where . . .*

He sang those simple lines over and over, and the baby laughed and sucked his fists until his eyes looked swollen and wet with sleep. "Where did you learn that?" I asked.

"Your mother has taught me a few things," he boasted.

"So she has." I tried to avert my eyes, but caught a glimpse of him then, and behind the counter at work that night I saw him again and again in the faces of customers who called for ketchup and coffee. Maybe he was on my mind, but most likely the mistake was due to his stature: there was nothing about his features that reminded me of anyone I knew, and so he could have been anyone. That night I found myself humming children's songs, and those simple melodies brought me back to a time I had all but forgotten. I was a young child when my father Isamu died, but I am sure he sang to me at bedtime.

It was close to midnight by the time I finished my shift, and I tiptoed to Goro's room, the way I did every night, to avoid waking anyone. All the lights in the house were off, which made me think everyone had gone to bed, but when I peeked into the baby's room I could see a shadow hovering over the crib. I was startled but not scared because I knew it was D. He walked briskly over to where I stood and pressed the door shut behind me. "Now that Goro is finally asleep I don't want to wake him."

"I see," I whispered, "I'm sorry if he disturbed you."

"Not at all." He smelled of shaving soap and exotic cigars.

"Good night, then." With my head bowed I reached for the doorknob, avoiding his eyes.

"I got up because I couldn't sleep."

I stopped. His face was only inches away from mine and I dared not move, could not breathe. "Good night," he whispered, and I felt his lips graze my cheek. Or maybe I was imagining, because when I finally looked up he had passed through the doorway and disappeared up the stairs.

That night I stood beside the crib watching the baby's chest rise and fall, but my thoughts were not focused on my son. D.'s rich smell lingered in the air and I felt flattered by his attention. He was my mother's husband and I had never known my own father; I was seventeen years old with a child who had only me to protect him, and D.'s kiss promised love, and safety. But I was wrong to be excited. In the weeks that followed, his flirtation became less discreet, and my response changed quickly from admiration to numbness. *I left Sadamichi because I had my son to consider and I'm in my mother's house because I have nowhere else to go.* When D. appeared in Goro's room I let him embrace me there, by the crib, and in my room with my mother sleeping directly above. I let his hands explore my body through the sheerness of my dress. *I am the light bulb beneath its shade, dark now, cold.* I didn't try to stop him; I even fantasized about my mother alone in her bed.

Nomi sits by my bedside perched on the chair as if it will no longer hold her. She is restless, and as she talks she fingers her long hair. She combs it behind her shoulders, then down over her face, then back over her shoulders again until all at once the water on my dresser goes flying and in one swift gesture she rises from the chair and lifts the red hem of her dress to mop up the mess.

"That's okay." *She is herself again, so eager to fix what is wrong.*

"No," she cries. "Oh, no."

With her back turned to me I cannot help noticing her slender legs. *She must have gotten them from her mother, thin, and so straight.* "Don't ruin your dress. Why don't you get a towel?" Accidents happen and I am not worried because whatever is left out can get wet, but suddenly I jump up and run to the bathroom, remembering the photographs. Sandwiched beneath the sheet of glass that Tadashi had fitted over the dresser top are all the precious memories I've got, and they will be destroyed if they get wet.

Standing over the sink I force myself to be still for a minute because my heart is beating so rapidly. I take a hand towel from the rack and use it to wipe away the sweat that has suddenly collected on my forehead and above my lip. I know it's not Nomi's fault. I haven't even looked at those pictures in years—haven't needed to because I've memorized every one by heart—still, I am as aware of their presence in my room as I am of my own existence.

When I return Nomi has cleared everything off my dresser. Now I look with her at so many snapshots suddenly made visible beneath water-stained glass. There is one of Tadashi holding Nomi and Melodie on each knee, one of Goro at four, one of me carrying Nomi at her second birthday party. "Who's that?" she wants to know.

"That's you."

"It couldn't be," she says, "that baby is so ugly."

"She is not." I bend over to examine the photo carefully with my magnifying lens and it brings back happy times. My eyes are open wide and I am standing perfectly straight and proud to be holding my granddaughter.

Nomi lifts the edge of the glass and pulls the picture free. "Can I have it?"

"Of course." I cannot refuse her, although I'd rather keep it safe under the glass.

Holding the cardboard photo in the middle, Nomi rips it in half, then quarters, then drops them into the trash can beside my bed. "What an awful picture," she says, "could you imagine how embarrassing it'd be if anyone saw it?"

"But I liked it," I sigh.

"Ooops." Her voice rings falsely, and a little too loud.

"It's one of the only good pictures of me I've seen."

"Oh." Now she bites her lip like she's going to cry and I could kick myself for saying anything.

"How's school?" I ask.

"Okay."

"And Eric?"

She shrugs. Then her body begins to tremble and a sob escapes from her throat. "I'm sorry I haven't been down to visit you," she says at last.

"It's okay." I close my eyes. "I know you're busy these days."

"I'm not too busy."

She pats my hand, but it is not all right. She no longer needs me—I realize it now—*she has become me*, and I feel for the first time truly afraid. Nomi leaves to change out of her wet dress and I close the thick orange drapes over the windows because I desire darkness. Evening voices, morning light slowing in the afternoon—I want to hear quiet, but even in darkness I can decode the pattern of footsteps, interpret the meaning of hushed silences. I know a few things about deceit.

The winter of '41 I turned twenty-one and war was declared. Late that spring, on a gray afternoon, I boarded a train behind my mother, with Goro in my arms, and I did not feel scared or sorry to be leaving. If there was dread in my heart that day it was because of a sudden insight I had. As the San Francisco landscape flattened into groves of barren trees, I had a premonition that my mother's house would be there with D. standing like a flapping tongue in its doorway to swallow us down when we returned.

At Heart Mountain, my mother and I shared a barrack with the Tanizaki couple and their daughter Kiko, a sweet teenaged girl who helped take care of Goro. I wonder what ever happened to her. Sleeping, eating, even going to the bathroom, Kiko would always appear with that cheerful laugh of hers. And while everyone complained about the lack of privacy, it did not bother me; I even felt protected in the presence of so many others. What I minded about camp had mostly to do with my mother. For three, almost four years, she and I were hardly ever parted and she spoke then endlessly, vituperatively, about D. "That no good hakujin bastard, I bet he's sold the house and moved to Canada with all my things." She talked this way whenever the Tanizakis were out, or if they were there she whispered. "I should have guessed that this would happen from the start."

She went on until one evening before dinner—the Tanizakis had left and Kiko had taken Goro—I asked her what difference it would have made if D. did sell the house and leave with her things. "If it weren't him then there'd be someone else, you know that. But you're lucky to have him." I savored the irony of my remark.

"You think I'm lucky, do you?" She had been styling her hair for dinner as if the mess hall were some fancy restaurant, but now she hovered just inches from my face and lowered her voice to a whisper that made me shudder. "Well, you had your own reasons for wanting him to stick around."

"I don't know what you're talking about." I backed away, knew then that she knew, and that I must never, never give in to her. "It is ludicrous to think D. will run off with your house."

My mother glared at me, magnifying the awkwardness of my remark under her gaze. I knew she knew I had betrayed her and now I was protecting a man who had violated me, but under her gaze I was made meaner, bigger by her own making. "Isn't it enough for you to be able to keep what is yours when others have lost everything?"

She went back to fixing her hair, allowing her silence to shrink me. Then, her back turned to me, she muttered, "You have always wanted what is mine and now you have spoiled any chance I've ever had for love."

I had witnessed her vain jealousy before, but was she justified this time? Her long black hair—she had tied it behind her. Immaculate, it shone in the style of elegant women from the Taisho era, only now the pins were coming loose; stray hairs sprang from the sides of her head, and each time she reached a hand up to tuck them back into place another one loosened. "What do you expect me to feel after you seduced him?"

My whole body went numb. *I am the light bulb beneath the shade. Dark and cold now shattered, she has known all along.* "What are you saying?"

"Don't pretend to be modest," she said. "He only put up with your clumsy attempts to please him because of me. He was a pervert, you know, and I had to force him downstairs to get him away from me." She was seething now, crushing me beneath her rage, forcing me back in time. A child's voice inside my head spoke: *There was a time when D. warmed me. He rocked me in his arms and whispered in my ear that he loved me and it could not be that she masterminded even that.* Now I was shivering so fiercely that my teeth chattered. I clenched my jaw shut against her accusations, but she did not stop.

"D. didn't love you." *You are evil,* her eyes said. And with those words spoken, she raised a hand to fasten one last pin in place and moved swiftly out the door.

6
.
N o m i

In the Berkeley Hills, in the backyard of her boyfriend, Richard, my sister sunbathes with her eyes closed, her chin tilted skyward; she is a beautiful statue and I am as invisible as the air around her. With my parents away for a week and Eric gone the whole summer I don't have anything to do, and Melodie reminds me of that by saying I am only allowed to go with her to Richard's if I behave myself: *stay out of my way, serve me drinks by the pool and talk to Richard so he'll leave me alone while I tan.* I feel sorry for Richard because he's in love. I see the way he looks at my sister and I know it's hopeless. She doesn't even notice him—it's like she's got her head somewhere way up in the clouds and he's practically drowning, calling her name, but she doesn't hear him.

An admirer of what he calls Melodie's exotic beauty, Richard talks a lot as he bakes himself in the sun, and I listen, wondering what he thinks of me. "Asian girls are so hot," he says. "Do you really think she likes me?" We watch from the deck as Melodie floats on a raft in her white bikini.

"What makes you think she would?" I like to give him a hard time.

Richard is not unattractive. He is nineteen, suntanned, tall, and a good swimmer, and toward evening when Melodie drives off to the Safeway for more Cokes and he asks me if I want to race him I agree. We decide on five laps freestyle, three breaststroke, and two underwater to finish it up, and when I come up panting behind him in the deep end he kisses me and I kiss him back. And when he wraps his strong legs around my bony hips and pries my bikini bottoms aside I don't protest. Sex with Richard is uncomfortable, but the pain is not unbearable. My body feels weightless underwater. I do not close my eyes. I watch the spotted shell of a ladybug drift by. She flutters her delicate red wings, drying them for flight, but all at once Richard makes a sharp lunge and she rises on a wave only to disappear.

I look for her under the water, then up in the air, and that's when I notice Melodie's feet. I am not sure whether I see her first, or she sees me, or how long she has been standing there.

Richard is the first to scramble over the side of the pool. "Melodie," he cries. "Melodie."

"Richard," my sister hisses.

Their voices sound funny as they call each other's names. I stand at my sister's side, across from Richard, who appears to have lost some brain cells. I want his mouth to open. I listen for the words that will make things right again, but he says nothing.

"What were you doing, Richard?" Melodie demands.

"Nothing." Richard speaks at last, but he is not believed. "Go inside NOW," she turns to me.

In the bathroom I pat myself dry with a large blue beach towel. I begin filling the basin with tap water to soak my suit because that is what I always do after a swim, but I am shivering when it's not even cold, wondering what happened to the ladybug—*she probably drowned*— when I should be thinking what to say to my sister, when Melodie spins me frantically around. My eyes are dry but hers are wet and swollen. "Are you okay?"

She is crying, but I wish she'd stop because I know her tears aren't for me. She doesn't care that Richard is in love with her, or know that I let Richard do to me what he wanted to do to her; she is crying because what she saw scared her, and aside from getting caught, I am not sorry.

The night my parents return, the four of us have dinner together as usual. My mother serves us salad, rice, and fish, and brags about how she played in the Monterey Bay golf championship and won a prize for putting closest to the tee. She disappears down the hall and comes back with a gold-plated club. "See there?" She waves it like a champion. My mother loves to win, but even more than that she loves prizes. I am reminded of Fourth of July picnics—the year I went into kindergarten she entered me in all the games. Her favorite was the three-legged race, and even though I was no match for her, I did my best to keep pace. *That's right,* she coached me. *We've got it now. Let's go! Don't look down at your feet. Look there, at the finish line.* She pointed and I followed her finger to where a row of people stood waving their arms, whistling. They frightened me, but more immediate was the throb in my ankle from the twine that tied it to my mother's. *Come on, Nomi,* she screamed, *faster, faster.* Nearing the end, I made the mistake of looking down at my red party dress and shiny black shoes. At the same instant, my face plunged into the muddy grass. I would have cried but my mother swept me up by the elbow and the next thing I knew I was tucked safely under her arm sailing across the finish line. "Hooray," she hugged me, "we've won first place!"

I am looking at my mother who is holding up her gold-plated golf club, her prize, when my father cuts in. "There's something we need to talk about, Nomi."

I suck on the end of my fork, focusing my eyes on the tabletop. I know it is not going to be good.

"While we were away," he pauses, "what happened with you and Richard?"

"Why don't you ask Melodie?" I say, since Richard is her boyfriend. "You always believe what *she* says."

He ignores my last remark. "I *have* asked Melodie."

"Then why are you asking me?"

"Because we want to hear what you have to say."

Six eyes await my reply, but I have no answer; six ears ring when I drop my fork on my plate. "Nothing happened, okay?"

No one moves. Does he expect a public confession? And for what? If my mother were to ask me, I might tell her. If my father weren't there I might be able to think back and at least say something. But I have no story for my father. Richard is lost somewhere inside my head. "Nothing," I repeat.

My mother collects the remains of my half-eaten dinner. I look across the table at Melodie, but she is chewing her food, pretending to be somewhere else. I don't know what she told him about that night, but it is clear she has betrayed me, and my mother is no help because she is busy at the sink. My father keeps his eyes on me, and I stare meanly back at him. *He does not deserve to know about me. He wants information served to him the way my mother serves him dinner.* "I have nothing to say. May I be excused?"

"No," my father says and I should have known I wouldn't get off so easy. I roll my eyes and hum. *Tonight's the night, it's gonna be all right.* I do this to irritate my father, but his response is not what I expect.

"Your mother and I went away because I needed to think," he says. "I've decided to leave the church, so I thought you should know."

He thought we should know. I don't want to know this at all, and besides, what does his leaving have to do with Richard? Now my father, great messenger of revelations, has tears in his eyes. "I'm sorry," he says.

"Why are you sorry?" Melodie is suddenly back at the table and her question is genuine.

My father's shoulders collapse in a way that both terrifies and repulses me. "Because I didn't leave years ago. Because I'm leaving at all."

"That's okay," Melodie says. The word cryptic pops into my head, though I can't think what it means.

The phone rings and Melodie goes to answer it. It's probably Richard, wanting to know if she's free for a swim.

I am about to ask, again, to be excused, but before I can say anything my father rises from his chair and bends over to embrace me. His breath is hot and wet against my cheek and I turn away. This isn't right. It isn't right at all. A few feet away I can see my mother standing at the sink washing dishes. Her back is to me, but I know she can see what's going on. She has probably seen it coming all week, and now she stands with her back to me and I am trapped.

I want to walk through my room, out my window, and

keep moving. I will travel by foot as far as the shore and then I will swim. I hate the church, hate everything about it, but I hate my father more for wanting to leave it because somehow I am implicated in all this, and what I want most is to be left alone. Asleep that night I dream I am standing inside a locked window, high above the water and helpless I am watching someone drown.

You are hidden to me, but I think of Japan daily now. It is my first thought when I wake up in the morning, and throughout the dreary fall and winter of my senior year, you are what keeps my feet moving from one class to the next.

Japan is my pact with my grandmother that neither of us mention: *I didn't have to play the piano, or visit her every day, but someone had to. Now I have to go there because I can't just let her die.* I have applied to colleges, received acceptances from a few, and been congratulated as if this were a good thing. I tell my mother that getting into colleges doesn't mean anything because I am going to Japan, but she says just you worry about graduating with A's, then we can discuss *it* with Daddy. I make her promise because I need to know she's on my side, but the truth is, the only reason she doesn't say anything to my father is because she wants to believe I'll change my mind.

I should be happy, I tell myself, there is a purpose to my life. At night I lie awake counting the boys I've done it with like sheep. Eric Kobayashi, Richard Swenson, Todd Larkin. That's three more than anyone I know, and by this time next year who knows how many more there will be. I try to imagine everything different, the way it will be in Japan, only lately something is wrong. Graduation is only a month away, and after that Japan, but for three days in a row now I've woken up with a sick feeling in my stomach and last night I counted on the calendar and my period is five days late. *It couldn't be. How could it possibly be?*

My mother always talks about how the mind controls the body. *If you would just go to bed early, eat sensibly, and think good thoughts throughout the day you'd feel better.* I spend two weeks making sure I am in bed by eleven o'clock each night and out the door, my stomach full, with plenty of time to get to school in the morning. Since Melodie was always the slow one and she is away this year at college, being punctual is not a problem. During the day I try to concentrate on what the teacher is saying. Usually I just wind up counting—Eric in front of the Arboretum and Richard in the pool and Todd so many times I lose track— but so what? After school I come straight home, and even though I sometimes can't bear to see her I go downstairs to visit Grandma Rio. My new boyfriend Todd thinks I'm cracking up. He leaps out at me from behind lockers, waits outside my last class each afternoon, and calls me more often than he should just to ask if I'm okay.

I tell him there is nothing to worry about until one

morning, a Saturday, I wake up feeling fine. I sit across the table from my mother and as I eat my cereal I fight the urge to tell her how well I feel. I want to tell her that what she has taught me actually works, that I have improved the quality of my thoughts and actions and that today, for the first time in two weeks, I feel happy to be alive. I want to say that there really is something to going to bed early and eating wisely, but I bite my lip because comments like these would only make her suspicious. I wish I could be certain what she does and doesn't know. For almost two weeks I thought about telling her, then stopped because I could never tell her. Now maybe there is nothing to say. She is a travel agent who has booked her friends on flights around the world but has never gone anywhere herself; now, if I play my cards right, she will use her free flights to buy my ticket to Japan. I have come to breakfast maybe even hoping to hear her tell me I am not going anywhere, but she has not noticed.

"Melodie called last night while you were out with Todd," she whispers so that Granny upstairs will not wake up. "She says to say hi to you."

"How nice." My voice comes out too loud.

"How is Todd?"

"Fine." Last night he drove me down Highway 1 to Half Moon Bay and we sat on the beach in our sweatshirts looking for sea lions. It was a cool thing for him to do, to drive me out of the city and down the coast just because after dinner I said I wanted to look for sea lions. But then there weren't any, and when we got back in the car and started making out I just couldn't do it. I don't feel so good, I told him, but he shut me up with a kiss. I'm so hot for you, he said, and he took my hand and slid it down to his cock—I swear the guy is a walking hard-on—and he said you can't just get me all hot like this and then say you don't feel good. Don't, I said. What I really wanted to do was tell him what I've been so worried about, but he said I'll make you feel better.

"I thought we'd make some cookies today to send to her." Now my mother is staring at me funny.

"That sounds nauseating." I eye her. *Does she know?*

"I thought you loved cookies."

"I do." *What is wrong with her?*

"Chocolate chip or oatmeal?"

"Why not both?" From across the table I feel mean, derisive. If I rub my hands in the soft dough will my sister catch whatever I have? I smile at my mother, sure she will know what is happening and take back her offer, but she only nods. "Okay," she says.

I have always thought of my mother as being so observant, but maybe there are some things she does not want to know. Or maybe she does know. It is impossible to tell. Outside the window a huge yellow grasshopper is trying to get inside. He has his legs hooked in the screen and he is climbing up and down looking for an opening. I think of Todd again, moving in and out of me, and all I could say was it isn't safe. It isn't safe, you know.

"I just remembered," I whisper to my mother across the table. "I told Marni I'd spend the day with her."

"Oh." She is disappointed. Suspicious? "You haven't spent the day with her in a long time."

I haven't thought of my best friend, Marni, lately at all. "I'd better call her," I say.

The morning sky is gray, but there is no fog, and the waves swell in white peaks and roll into shore. Last night I sat on the shore watching them with Todd, and then all through breakfast with my mother I have been watching the way they rise up, thinking I am pregnant. I just know I am. Now I can't remember my best friend's number, but my fingers push the right buttons despite my doubts, and Marni answers. "Nomi? Nomi who?"

"Very funny," I tell her, *it's true, I must be,* and then I hear my own voice and the urgency is gone. "I guess I dialed the wrong number."

"Oh that Nomi." Marni pauses. "How are you?"

"Fine," I say. Then remembering, "Not so good."

"You can come over if you're not doing anything."

She is my best friend because she says what I most need to hear.

My mother offers to drive me because the Sadlers live in the Fillmore District, more than a mile away, but fortunately, because I don't think I could bear sitting next to her, she agrees with me when I say I need the exercise. Once I'm sure I can't be seen from the window, I make myself run as fast as I can down the hill. I run until sweat stings every pore in my face and air pumps through my lungs so fast I feel delirious. I do not stop for oncoming cars, or pause to let old people and dog walkers pass more easily. I run all the way through Huntington Park, past Grace Cathedral to St. Francis Memorial Hospital, where I stop along the grassy path and heave a milky stew of half-eaten cornflakes into the bushes.

Bent at the waist, hugging myself, strings of vomit attach me to my feet. Now I know it's true. It doesn't matter what I think or how hard I run, you have a heart of your own, inseparable from mine, and I have never felt so clear. I want to lie in the grass, close my eyes, dream, but as soon as I can catch my breath my feet lead me back to the path. You may have your own heart, distinct from mine, but my feet are still my own, and they cannot be stopped.

Marni's house looks just like the many other box houses surrounding it, only it's pale yellow and has an elaborate alarm system. The Sadlers moved into the city a couple of years ago when Marni's father was appointed head of pediatrics at St. Francis. Their house is nothing like ours, though, an old Victorian which Granny's father bought at the turn of the century. Upstairs Dr. Sadler is reading the morning paper, but he puts it aside and holds his arms out to me. "Nomi," he calls. "It's so good to see you." I veer left then right thinking he will guess if he gets too close, but he ruffles my hair and grins. "You're looking as pretty as ever. How are you?" *He doesn't know. He is a pediatrician and he doesn't know a thing!* Then Mrs. Sadler comes in drying her hands on a kitchen towel. "Hi, Nomi," she sings, and still holding the towel she kisses me noisily on both cheeks. Marni is there too, good old Marni, but once we're outside she acts funny. "What's wrong?" She holds her hand in front of her mouth. *She knows!*

"Can you tell?" I ask.

"Tell what?" She looks puzzled.

"Nothing," I say.

"Was it my parents?" she asks. "They can't seem to keep their hands off . . ."

"No." Now I must tell her. "I'm pregnant."

"What?" Marni hugs me. "Oh, Nomi, this is awful."

Awful?

"What do you want to do?"

"I don't know." *I'm going to have a baby.* A black car slows as it approaches the house, then passes.

"Of course you do." She looks me straight in the eye. "Have you told Todd?"

"No."

"Well, I can find out the name of a clinic." Because of

her father she has grown up accustomed to the physicality of life. I don't want her to *do* anything, but she has bright green eyes that sparkle when the sun hits them and I trust her.

"Don't tell Todd," she says all of a sudden.

"Why not?"

"If you tell him you're pregnant, he'll tell one of his friends. Then everyone will know."

"If I have a baby then everyone will know for sure."

Marni stops walking. "You're not serious, are you?"

"Maybe," I muse.

"Going through with this would force you to give up every dream you've ever had. You've got to have an—a—uhm—termination."

"You're right," I hear myself say. She does not know about you, or about Japan, still, termination thuds in my ear like a door slamming shut on my life. I know that this is called irony, that without it I would have no life to speak of. No Japan. No you. I am not shutting the door, I am opening it. Still, I worry.

Marni holds my hand as we walk and for a while neither of us says anything. I touch my free hand to my stomach and imagine two little eyes and a beating heart.

"So when did you find out?" Marni breaks the silence.

"Just this morning."

She nods. "Todd is such an asshole," she says. "He should have used something." She assumes that my predicament is his fault, that I am pregnant because my boy-friend is an asshole. She does not know that I seduced Eric, or what happened with Richard, and now Todd. I could never tell her that maybe I wanted this to happen. I let her believe I am innocent because I need her on my side.

Marni has recently gotten her license so she drives, and along the way neither of us says anything. Not for any lack of antiseptic the clinic smells dank inside; there is moisture trapped beneath the carpet, and under the floor-boards, and I imagine rivers of water. Like a sudden flood, the nurse sweeps in. She calls me into a small office with walls that reach only halfway to the ceiling, asks if I've ever been pregnant before, if anyone in my family has or has had cancer, diabetes, high blood pressure. I can hear my voice chanting no, no, no, no.

I give her the date of my last menstrual period. Then she gives me a plastic cup and tells me to bring back a urine sample, and after returning from the bathroom I wait alone in the room with the half walls where voices, some-times in Spanish, sometimes sobbing, always unrecogniz-able, march on like an underwater parade. I, alone, feel nothing, except that I am about to disappear, and if any-one were to touch me I think I'd strangle them. *You are all I have, and I will always protect you.* I wish it could be over with, and yet I don't know why I am here at all.

After what seems like forever the nurse knocks, then lets herself in. "Well, I have good news," she smiles. "You're not pregnant."

"Oh?" It is all I can manage. I do not feel relieved, I do not feel anything. "Can I sit here for a few more minutes?" I ask.

"Sure," she says, "but there are other people who need to use this room so don't be too long."

Don't be too long, there are other people to consider besides yourself. Why can't you think of the next person? Her voice stings me, or maybe it's my mother I am hearing.

In the waiting room Marni greets me with sorrowful eyes. "Are you okay? Do you want to sit down for a minute?"

"No, I've been . . ." Her face has no color. No color at all, except big green watery eyes. "Never mind."

"You've been crying, haven't you." She wraps her arms around me and I can feel the tears trapped like so much weight behind my eyes. "It's okay, Nomi," she says. "Was it horrible?"

I know she doesn't know there was no baby. *No me, you are dead.* How could she know? But how could I tell her? "Let's get out of here," I say, and as we walk back to the car a cramp seizes me, then releases, and the blood begins to flow.

■　■　■

On the longest day of the year I am lying on the grass in the backyard in my swimsuit, trying to get a tan and wondering what made me think I could live in Japan, let alone by myself, let alone plan my life. I am thinking what an idiot I have become and wondering what will happen to me now when I hear the thumping of heavy shoes and then my name. "Nomi"—it's my father—"come inside. I'd like to have a talk with you."

Slitting my eyes against the glare of the afternoon sun, I see him. He is dressed in a navy sport shirt and khaki trousers and his face is shadowed by a white envelope which he holds across his forehead. I half-expect him to bend over and try to embrace me, since that is his newest habit, and one that makes me cringe. But today he is my old father again, the same man who used to greet me every day as if meeting me for the first time. I can see my half-naked body in the lenses of his thick glasses and I wonder if he knows how awkward I feel. Staring up at him staring down at me, I decide he must, and I hate him.

"I'll be waiting for you in my study," he says.

When the sliding glass door shuts I count the seconds it will take my father to pass through the kitchen, down the hall into his study. Then I close my eyes. Holding my breath I dive into an imaginary pool of water and swim underwater laps until my lungs feel like bursting. Then I wrap my towel around my waist and walk calmly inside.

The house is cool and dark compared to outside. I

stand in front of my dresser, waiting for my eyes to adjust, then I brush my hair, dress in cut-offs and a T-shirt, and take a deep breath which I exhale all the way to my father's study.

Seated behind his desk, stacks of files laid out like a deck of oversized playing cards in front of him, my father is the dealer. All he lacks is a visor, and one of those funny black aprons they use at the casinos to hold change. "Is there something you'd like to tell me?" he begins. *Hit or hold.*

"No." *Hold, definitely hold.*

He rises from his chair and I duck, expecting him to strike me, even though he never has; he is standing to get the best possible view of my face when he slides my mail across his desk.

The letter is from a youth hostel in Japan responding to an inquiry I'd sent. "Don't act so surprised."

I can tell he feels satisfied, *he has dealt himself a winning hand*, but I am no longer numb. "Why did you open my mail?"

My father sits down again. He turns away and for quite a while he says nothing. Then, when I have almost forgotten what I'd asked him, he responds, "I thought it was for me."

I keep my eyes focused on the paper in front of me. "It has my name on it."

"Don't try to change the subject." He shakes his head. "The point is that this is the first I've heard of any of this."

He is right. A good daughter, someone like my older sister Melodie, always consults her father before making plans. Even before he says it I can hear his words, You're impossible . . . Take Melodie . . . If you had consulted me first . . . You're out of line.

Even if he did truly mistake my mail for his own . . . If he had . . . I keep staring at the paper in front of me because I need to be reminded what the real problem is. *Can't he help me out here?* "You have no right to open mail addressed to me."

"If I hadn't opened your mail how would I have known?"

I have no answer for him. I never wanted to tell him, and yet I wish suddenly he could have known all along. "I've been meaning to tell you for some time now." I say this slowly, deliberately.

"You have?"

"Yes."

My father swivels around in his chair and I notice a bald spot there, in the back, and how he brushes his hair to cover it up. I have rehearsed in my mind all the angry words we might exchange, only now that the moment has come there is nothing to say. "Once you finish your education you can go wherever you want—"

"Thank you," I interrupt, "but I can't wait that long."

"Why not?"

"Because I can't." Feeling the tears come, I take a deep breath.

"You haven't thought this out," he says. "Even if you found a place to stay, how would you get around? You don't even know the language. And what did you think you'd do with your time. Have you looked into colleges? I'm sorry, Nomi, but you're still a minor and you can't just go around making these decisions by yourself. Besides, how did you think you'd support yourself?"

"I saved lots of money working at the Baskin-Robbins last summer . . ."

He laughs. "We want you to go to college in California."

"I can't do that."

"Why not?"

I have no answer. "Because I can't."

When my mother's car pulls into the garage the whole house is deadly quiet. I have been sent to my room, and listening through the wall I am reminded of a night long ago when I woke up to the sound of angry voices coming from my parents' room. Finding their door locked I crawled back to my room; I was old enough to walk, but young enough to cuddle close to the wall and listen for Melodie's breathing on the other side. I imagined myself to be the subject of that first argument, and later Melodie told me she thought the same thing. But this time she is gone. I have sworn my mother to secrecy, and she has kept her promise.

My mother knows how to keep a secret; she knows

about deceit. She can spot a liar a mile away, but she isn't opposed to what she calls "white lies." She once showed me how red can become pink with a dab of white, and that white lies are not a bad thing. Though she isn't a painter, my mother is the one who taught me to mix colors, never mixing any herself, and now she must think of something to say to my father.

As far as I know, my parents do not exchange angry words, only silence, which is probably the best weapon of all. When I stumble into the kitchen late that night I see my father's head bent low over our kitchen table and across from him my mother perfectly still, and her sorrow breaks my heart. I take a seat next to her because I want to defend her. I want an explanation, I want forgiveness, but when no one looks up I return to my room. I may have to wait forever, and for a long time I lie awake listening to their silence.

7
.
R i o

Nomi is gone, not to Japan as she had wished—she will spend this year at college in California, a compromise—but next year, the year after, who knows? She writes to me:

It's nice here. Don't tell anyone I said that because then they'll think I'm liking it, and sometimes I do, but not always. My new boyfriend is a senior named Porter. He lives off campus in an apartment that overlooks the East Bay, and I take the train there sometimes on weekends because it's too noisy to try to study in the dorms. Sometimes, though, he comes to see me and we go for long walks. The campus is huge—big buildings everywhere just like a cement forest and just when you think you're lost there's Campanile tower forever pointing north. There's also this one footbridge strung together with all these thin planks of wood and when you walk across it creaks and moans like it's going to collapse any minute. It's on my way to the library, and every time I go to study I bring a penny with me and stand in the middle of the bridge and let it fall and make a wish for you. I hope you're happy and things are good at home.

Porter isn't really my boyfriend. I like him a lot, but I think of him mainly as a good friend, and someone who can tell me all about Japan because he was there once because his father was in the military. Do you know he says the streets in Tokyo have no names, and they all wind into each other. When you want to know how to get somewhere they draw you a map. Tizu o kaku, they say. He's got a whole drawer full of maps he saved and they're just wild. I hope no one ever asks me for one, though, because you know I can't draw! But I'm only with Porter some of the time, and other times it gets very, I don't know, lonely. And I guess I'm telling you this because I figured you'd know what I mean. I don't know how to say this but you and I always tell each other things and I keep wondering if that's how you felt. When I was much younger didn't you once try to kill yourself? I don't mean to be morbid, and I hope this doesn't upset you, but I need to know. Write me back if you feel like it, but if you don't I'll write to you again anyway.

I read the last part again and again until the page flops over itself. I am limp. *Didn't you once try to kill yourself?* What does she mean to ask? She will never be alone. Even I

know that unhappiness does not approach out of nowhere. But does she fear loneliness because of me? At
night in her dreams does she fall forever downward? Like
me, does she wake up sucking blood from her cheek?

It's a mother's job to make the world safe for her children. Tomoe is a good mother, and that's how I know I am
the one to blame. Not that Goro isn't a good son. But
didn't I poison Goro, and isn't that why he has failed to
protect Nomi? Goro never talks about the past. The time
before he met Tomoe is a chasm too deep to be crossed,
or maybe it is just that he has forgotten. If so, who can say
it isn't better that way? But I remember. I never had the
proper, maternal feelings for him. When he was pulled
from my body, handed to me wrapped in a blanket, his
face red with blood, my pulse did not quicken the way
Tomoe's did when she held her daughters for the first
time. I saw the way she loved them. There was relief, yes,
that he was no longer a part of me, no longer feeding off
my body, but my heartbeat slowed then. His weight, so
solid against my breasts, spoke not of new life, but of new
burdens and old, failed dreams.

I came to the conclusion that I would end my life on a
sunny afternoon in winter, a day I'd been working up to
for a long time. Tadashi came home with storm windows,
which he said he got to shut the draft out of the downstairs part of the house, but they let in only the tiniest

amount of air and I suspect that's what it must feel like to fly in one of those big jets, to hear the constant whirring and buzzing of pressurized air. When I complained that there wasn't enough air, Tadashi said he'd spent all that money trying to keep out the draft; he'd only done it because he thought it would make me feel better, but if I wasn't happy I could just lift them a little. He showed me how to push the window up by pressing the two levers at the bottom, but he did not understand that I couldn't breathe at all. All night I'd gasp for air until in the morning Tadashi would come. He'd open the window, let in the light, but still there was no air.

The next thing I knew he was hanging that heavy, rust-colored drapery. I remember when Nomi first saw those drapes she called them dragon wings. Those dragon wings meant it was always night and I no longer cared about time. Then I began visiting an old part of the country in my sleep; maybe it was Japan. I can't be sure since I've never been there, but I found myself wandering through an apple orchard where the trees had been hit by a frost because I could see that they were brown and withering. Their leaves and fruit had fallen prematurely and rotting apples lay on the ground in every direction. I was barefooted and the soft fruit oozed beneath me, but as I walked on I saw that a few of the apples looked edible, so I lifted my skirt into a pouch and began collecting the reddest ones. I knew that my destination was a wooden shack—I could see it off in the distance—but I took my time getting there, stopping more than once to pick up the reddest apples and turning back a couple of times to get a better look at the groves of withering trees as I climbed a steep hill. When I got closer to the shack I could see my mother standing in front of a splintery door. I felt amazed that I could see her at all, given my poor vision, but suddenly everything was clear—clearer than it had ever been. I could see the grains and knots in the wood on the door, its handle made out of bone, and most clearly my mother's face, shriveled and fierce. "Faster, faster." She was waving violently with her arms. She remained just outside the door frame. I knew she was not dead; she was there to trick me and I did not want to go to her, but one by one apples began tumbling out of my pouch, and as they fell to the ground a kind of lightness overcame me. My legs moved faster and faster until I was lifted off the ground and the wind behind me grew strong enough to carry my body forward.

I'd gone that far when Nomi appeared beside my bed. It was as if she'd entered my dream, only I was awake then, feeling her hand pressed inside mine. She didn't say anything to me at first, let me wake up slow to find her there, framed by a box of light that escaped through the drapes. My impulse was to ask her about my vision, see if she'd had it too, but she was so small, her seventh birthday barely past, and as I awoke all I knew was that I longed to feel that sensation again, and from then on I understood what needed to be done. I'd understood nothing, until suddenly everything came clear. My simpleminded belief that what I needed was oxygen wasn't true. Without air to breathe, everyone I loved and hated would not cease to exist—only I would be as silent as a rock and darker than the deepest cave, and the world would go on unbound by my love and hate. But the next thing I knew, Goro was pointing to the clear-paned window beside my bed and twisting the doorknob back and forth. I remember the first words he spoke to me, when I was cognizant enough to know whom he was talking to. "No bars on the windows, no locks on the doors." It was an odd thing to say to a person who was not curious enough to care, and it stuck with me because I knew then how much he hated me. Now I was the child, peering helplessly through metal bars at him, the way he had once looked to me for protection through the slatted wall of his crib. He'd held his arms up to me, and now my arms were strapped to my sides.

Those days so much was clear, and yet I was blind. Because of some rule, I wasn't allowed to wear my corrective lenses, and without them I couldn't keep track of my glasses. I'd feel my way over the table beside my bed, sticking my hand in a glass of water, knocking over a book, a bed tray, a pot of flowers, which would send a nurse rushing to my bedside. "What's the problem here, Rio?" she'd ask.

"I'm trying to find my glasses."

"Well, you're wearing them, dear."

And there I'd be. I'd reach my hand up only to find my glasses hanging from the bridge of my nose. The drugs blurred my vision, or so they said. But the real problem is that I need both my glasses and the lenses to see at all. Why couldn't they understand that?

It wasn't the drugs. I can still remember a conversation I overheard between my doctor and my son. "She was an only child," Goro volunteered. "Her father died when she was young."

"At what age?"

"I don't know exactly. One, maybe two."

"I see. Of what?"

There was the silence of days passing. Amazing, too, how quickly I could travel all those long years back to the place where no time has passed at all. All those long years back while I waited for Goro to respond.

"Natural causes," he said.

The silence that followed crackled in my ears like an avalanche, and the years tumbled down. Why should he lie? My mother killed my father, and even my son, the minister, did not have the power to absolve her. That was why, just as soon as I was able to, I told Dr. Steiger how wrong Goro had been. My father hadn't died of natural causes: my mother had killed him.

"Do you think that your mother killed your father?" He was incredulous.

"Yes. I am positive that my mother's behavior led to my father's death."

"What type of behavior, exactly?"

"My mother was what Japanese call kichigai."

"I'm sorry. I don't know what that means."

"Crazy, only worse."

"I see. Can you tell me a little more?"

I shook my head because there was nothing more to say. There is no way to make the past right. My father knew this. He was such a kind, gentle spirit. He never minded being judged. Still, I had to sit on my hands to stop them from shaking. There is so little I believe in this life, and yet I believed this: I needed to protect my father because he couldn't protect himself. At the same time, it was rage that pinched my throat closed, and hatred that burned my eyes and finally made me shut them, hoping the questioning would end there. But of course it didn't. It went on that way, with Dr. Steiger prodding me. That's why I never told him about my dream. Not because I did not sense it was significant, but because he didn't deserve to know about me. My dreams are not something I share with strangers.

He always wanted a little more, just a few more details, but like a child at the seashore, he could have bailed the sand out of my soul until his hands were raw, only to end up with water and more water everywhere. From him

I learned the unmistakable shame involved in having to justify my life to a stranger. The private humiliation of being locked up because I wanted to die, only to face my husband Tadashi, my son, his good wife Tomoe, and know a different kind of shame because the desire for an end to my life had not left me. There was the vague recognition of having come so close to meeting my mother in death and knowing then that she still lived—the waking from the death I had desired as a way to leave my mother only to be more certain than ever that neither death nor life would ever separate me from her. And then there was the daily bearing of tonsils, chest, and buttocks for clinicians who thought that if they could shine a light down my throat and magnify my tonsils, x-ray my chest, or inject me with a new drug, they could cure once and for all my desire.

I remember how incredulous Dr. Steiger sounded when he said, *So you think your mother killed your father. Could you tell me a little more.* About my mother, Tadashi, Goro, Tomoe, even Melodie and Nomi. What could he possibly have been looking for?

Anyone could have told him that there are enough worms to eat the heart out of any childhood. I could have told him about the apples I had seen in my dream, about their decay: overripened, half-eaten, worm-bitten. *I had picked only the purest, reddest ones and lifted my dress into a pouch to carry them.* If he had asked even once—not about my mother, not about my past, not about my day—if he had really wanted to know, maybe then, just maybe I would have told him. I could have told him how once I loved a man whose name no one mentions, even though I have lived with the memory of him daily for nearly forty years. I could have told him how good it once felt to be whole.

But I know what he would have thought. Goro's mother is mad as a hatter—delusional, I think is the word they use. Maybe there is nothing to tell. I loved him, that is all.

Nomi speaks of the bridge, the one she walks every day. *A footbridge, strung together by thin planks of wood, in a concrete forest. When you walk across, it creaks and moans and I throw a pebble in, luck for you, as if it's going to collapse any minute.* Maybe you don't know, Nomi, that I walk that bridge every day. I am there, right alongside you. I see, even more clearly than you, the length of cable connecting one plank to the next, the rust forming there, cracks in the wood weakening it ever so slightly. But exactly how much will it sway, then give before it snaps, I cannot tell you.

You see, back at Heart Mountain no one wanted to know me. I was a divorced woman with a child and the other single women preferred the company of my elegant mother, the proper, well-mannered woman whose mere presence suggested promises and secrets, and who, when she shouted obscenities at me, gave them something to talk about. I used to say to myself: who could blame them for hating me? But then I blamed them. I hated them all. Maybe even more than I shrank at my mother's rantings I hated their whispering behind my back. *What an unfortunate position to put a child in,* they'd say. *Poor thing.* Even more than my dislike of them, I despised their pity.

I did not need their pity, though I pitied myself. I was pitifully lonely, and I knew even then that my hatred of them was the only thing that kept me alive, prevented me from turning inward.

Then Kenji came to me. Toward the end of that first summer when not even my mother was speaking to me. Too good even to look at me, she had hung a white sheet between her bed and mine, and when she wanted something, or to see her grandson, she would pop her head around. But that afternoon my mother was teaching tea ceremony to a group of newly promised brides and the face that appeared from behind that white sheet was not hers. I remember the perspiration beaded above his lip and dripping down the sides of his face—even before I turned around to see him standing there, the sweet smell of his sweat breaking through the arid heat.

Is it that way for you too, Nomi? Do you smell first what your eyes are slow to reveal?

He wears a white undershirt stained wet across the chest. "May I come in?"

His voice is tentative, but his eyes are undiluted, fixed

on me in such a direct way that I turn to see if there might be someone else behind me. *Goro is asleep there, sprawled in only his underpants across the bed, not him. But me?* "Who are you looking for?"

"I'm taking a survey for the *Heart Mountain Sentinel*," he says. "May I come in?"

"Oh," I whisper, indicating with my eyes my son asleep behind me. "Yes, come in." I pat the edge of the bed and motion for him to sit. I am about to apologize that there is no chair, *there is barely enough space to sit and the air in the room is dizzying and close, I should stand and allow him some room*, but no, I refuse to apologize, or stand in this heat, or back away.

I expect, at any moment, that he will say, "When is Reiko coming back? It's her I've come to speak with." But he does not ask about her, does not rise to leave when I do not mention her. He does not ask about my mother or mention the survey again. I watch him carefully as the wet spot on his shirt spreads, and under my arms and the soles of my feet feel hot, but he does not mention the heat. Instead he wants to know where I am from. How long have I been here? Where do I plan to go when I am set free? What do I miss most about my life before I came here?

I tell him I don't miss anything. And when he looks at me doubtfully, I say, "I'm not lying."

"Maybe," he says, "it's that you don't want to see. Maybe you don't think about the things you miss so that you will not be miserable. If so, that is not a bad way to be."

"No, that's not it." I pause. "It's that I don't really think much about anything."

"I see." He places his hands on his knees as if to rise, and my hands instinctively cover my chest. I have exposed something of myself, *the pins holding my dress together, a dress that isn't even mine and hangs noticeably over the hollows of my body*. If I had any decency I'd turn from this man and run out the door, but something inside me sticks, *Goro's breathing, so slow and even behind me*, and I don't want him to leave.

"Are you married?" he asks, hands still on his knees.

"I'm divorced." A spell has been cast and now broken. The heat lifts. From the bottom of my feet out the top of my head it leaves my body like so much steam.

"I see." He squints, as if in recognition of some important fact. "I'm sorry to ask such a rude question, but I've noticed you before, and your son, and I've wanted to meet you for some time now."

"Oh?"

The room gets quiet except for breathing. Goro's, his, mine. I am flattered. "I saw in the newsletter that your mother is teaching tea ceremony this afternoon, and so I knew you'd be alone, and I hope it's all right with you that I've come here."

"Yes." I mean to say more. I'd like to ask where he is from, when he will come again, if he will stay. I think I know, but I need him to tell me why he's wanted to meet me so that later, when I am alone, I can repeat his words to myself.

"Kenji Yamashiro." He holds his hand out. "Nice to meet you."

"I'm Rio—" I pause. Should I use Miyazawa, my father's name, the name that was mine until I married Sadamichi? Or Tanaka, my married name? I swallow hard, feeling a sudden urge to invent a new name for myself. Who would know my secret here, among so many strangers? "Kobata," I say, "I'm Rio Kobata."

And when he goes, I can't say if I am relieved or sorry, only that I am alone.

It's after that first meeting that I begin to walk. I leave Goro with my mother, and I tell myself, *If I can just see Kenji today, if I can pass him while I'm out walking, then today will be fine.* I walk the length of the camp, past row after row of identical brown barracks. I kick up the dry earth pretending to enjoy the open air even though, because of my weak eyes, I can't see clearly past my own feet. It doesn't bother me that everything blurs like so much background; the colors remain the brown of earth and blue of sky, and there is comfort in that. But when Kenji joins me on my walks there is always something more—he points at a morning glory growing between a crack in the dirt, a badger hole and two sets of prints. Through his eyes a pile of small rocks becomes a garden, and when I am with him the landscape of Wyoming reveals itself before my eyes so that those first days of autumn will remain with me forever —the crackle of wind sweeping off the mountains and through the slatted wood barracks, the smell of burning pine and creosote from the mess halls, the canny, sweet smell of Kenji so close to me. And though the camp is situated on a low plain, there are mountains to the south, and I can look out through Kenji's eyes past the barbed wire and all that it contains.

Nomi writes:

> *Are you mad at me? Maybe this is silly but I thought by now you would have answered my letter. If I upset you I am sorry . . . Was it because I told you about Porter? Because he's a senior and I'm just a freshman? My friend Tasha, she says that college is about meeting new people. But don't worry because I'm studying too—school's the easy part. Write soon or I'm going to worry about you.*

I don't write back. I think of her daily, but I guess I don't have much to say.

The fact is, I never paid much attention to what I believed before Kenji. Before him I don't think I believed in anything. But then I believed in him, and when I was with him I believed in myself. Kenji loved what I loved, and maybe he loved me too, but then there was Tadashi, whom I met not long after I started seeing Kenji, and that is the other side.

One afternoon, while I was out walking in search of Kenji, Goro went out on his own, looking for me, and all that time I thought he was with my mother and she thought he'd gone off with me, and by the time he caught up with me I had met up with Kenji and apparently he had found Tadashi. Complicated. It all feels so complicated now, and yet what remains is a simple image: a small figure shadowed in the bright sunlight beneath a larger one—Goro approaching with Tadashi.

It turned out that Tadashi and Kenji were friends, and Goro quickly befriended Tadashi, and so naturally Tadashi became my friend too. And now I know what I couldn't have known then. I can see it all so clearly—that first chance meeting, there in the snow, that somehow familiar shape becoming near, narrowing into focus. Recognizing my son there, in the crook of Tadashi's arm, is like seeing my own life change. Introductions were made. I held out my hand and Tadashi shook it, and Goro held his hand out, and it was not difficult to see that he was fond of Tadashi. And I liked him too. There was something kind and gentle, almost simple, about the way he stood in the snow shaking hands, smiling.

But there is nothing simple about what happened next. Things got complicated somehow, and forty years later I have still not got it right.

What I wanted most that winter, and in the spring and

summer that preceded it, was for Kenji to ask me to marry him. Inside the barbed-wire fences, the days approached slowly, as if made timid by the war being fought on the outside. But the monotony only served to ridicule me. I knew the war would not last forever, and yet Kenji took his time—some days I would not see him at all. He'd spend the day writing an article, or helping to haul fire-wood. Other days my mother would insist that he stay and talk with her, or Goro would fuss and I would watch him across the room, a small space made enormous by his distance from me, and I would think: All this waiting, all this distance—is this life? Still, I waited. What choice did I have? What else was I going to do? I waited until the last possible moment, hoping he'd ask tomorrow, or the next day, or the next. Sometimes, it becomes clear to me that I am still waiting, though forty years later I am the fool. There was a time when I stopped waiting for Kenji and waited instead for death, but I have grown old, and that time has passed. Now the only punctuation marking an otherwise unremarkable procession of days is your occa-sional letter—letters you write, and letters you have writ-ten, which I take out and read from time to time.

You write:

Big trouble today. I told Porter I had a test tomorrow and needed to spend all night at the library so I could have dinner with this other guy who Tasha said really wanted to

take me out. He said that was fine, even wished me good luck,
so I thought everything was cool. But then I'm having dinner
at this really nice restaurant and guess who comes in? Porter's
Best Friend Ted. Can you believe it? I want to sink under the
table, and then I think maybe he won't see me because he's
sitting having drinks in the bar, but I'm not that lucky
because he sees me and comes over. Hi, Nomi, he says, real
nonchalantly like he doesn't even notice that the person next to
me is a guy and not Porter. So I think, fine, if it's okay with
you it's definitely okay with me, but when I get up after
dinner to go to the bathroom he's standing by the pay phone
and he puts his hand over the receiver and pulls me aside and
says not to worry, that he knows Porter thinks I'm at the
library but he won't tell, and that if I want to go out to
dinner with him next Friday that would be even better. Then
he pushes me up against the phone and spreads my legs apart
with his knee and kisses me on the mouth. Can you believe
that? I know you're my grandmother and so I probably
shouldn't even be saying stuff like this to you, but there's no
one else I can trust and I feel so, I don't know, dirty. I went
to the bathroom after that and washed out my mouth and
took a good hard look at myself in the mirror and said forget
it. I just kept saying that over and over. Then I walked back
out to where I'd been sitting and that idiot Tasha set me up
with had ordered baked Alaska and it was sitting on the table
in flames and we ate it and he didn't even ask what took me
so long.

*I hate everyone right now (except you, of course). I'm
ready to leave this place and never come back.*

You could be me in this letter—forty years ago. Your
letters tell a story. One that's yours, but also a version of
mine, happening this time to you, and because of you, to
me again.

I have known Rons, Darryls, Jeffs, Bens, have held the
hand of a faceless man with one of my hands; felt the thin
suspension rope cut into my palms until callouses grew
over each knuckle, and I can tell you that each time you
cross that bridge with someone different the journey becomes lighter, easier, only, like I say, the callouses form
like scar tissue over your heart, and that is what scares me.
I wonder, why did you go out with Ron, Darryl, Jeff, Ben,
or whatever his name is? You first wrote to me that you
and Porter were just friends, and if so why should it matter
that you go to dinner with someone else? If not, why
should you lie to me about Porter? Maybe it is the same
for you as it was for me. I waited for Kenji to ask me to
marry him, but when Tadashi proposed, I believed I did
not have a choice about marrying him. Just like I didn't
have a choice about marrying Sadamichi, or what happened between D. and me. It was too late to change a
pattern that had already taken shape. I had Goro, and I
wanted what was best for him. Time was running out, I
would never hand my son over to my mother, and alone

I could not provide for him. But who knows, maybe you don't love Porter the way I loved Kenji. I remember one afternoon when he and I were out walking. It was spring and the last bit of snow had finally melted away. We had been out for a while—long enough for the chilly April breeze to turn my ears numb—saying nothing to each other (me hoping of course that he was steadying himself to propose to me), when finally he broke the strained silence. "Rio, didn't you say your last name was Kobata?" Remembering the lie I had told, I said all I could say, "Yes, that's right." "But Tadashi says your last name is Tanaka." "Oh, if that's what Tadashi says."

I remember the suspicion in his eyes and how helpless I felt to assuage him. Even Kenji did not understand my need to reinvent myself, or how successful I almost was in his company. Maybe everyone needs to reinvent themselves, or maybe it is that you are collecting secrets of your own that you need to hide from. Is that why you asked, Nomi, what it was like for me back then? Well, it is too late for me.

Wondering how my life would have been different with my beloved will not do me any good, and yet I can't help but wonder. The night before my wedding when I lay crying in the bed next to my mother's she whispered through the sheet that I should be happy. As if to spite me she said, "Kenji has always known that Tadashi is fond of you. Maybe it was out of respect for Tadashi's feelings that he never proposed to you." That night my mother's words enraged me. I vowed not to forgive her, and yet I believed her and instead of blaming her I blamed Kenji and myself for the mistake I was about to make. Years later, when my mother saw how miserable I made Tadashi, she said it was my own selfishness that caused me to marry. It was as if she wanted me to know about her deceit, but it wasn't until years later that I put the pieces together and the other side came clear.

Tadashi knew how much I loved Kenji, and I became his friend because he was Kenji's friend and I could confide in him about Kenji. In confidence I told him my secret wish: *I know the war will not last forever, though I wish it would.* I wanted the war to go on and on to give Kenji and me the time we needed, but because I knew it wouldn't I entrusted Tadashi with my wish that Kenji would propose, and I believed in his tact, and in his ability to relay my secrets to my beloved.

Maybe I was naive, but I never believed that Tadashi's intentions were anything other than to bring me closer to Kenji. Because I didn't believe in myself I didn't believe Tadashi could have fallen in love with me, and when Hiroshima and Nagasaki were bombed and rumors spread that those left would be forced to leave camp in a matter of days, Tadashi was the one to propose. The turmoil was everywhere, and unable to see past my own misery, I believed he had proposed because he was sorry for me, and I accepted his proposal because I was sorry for myself.

Back then, I knew only my own story. I knew that I was miserable and that my one wish for myself would not be fulfilled, but I didn't understand why. It wasn't until the year I tried to end my life that Kenji resurfaced in the form of a letter. Twenty-eight years after the war, he had been diagnosed with some degenerative illness, and before he died he wrote to me to explain that he had asked my mother for permission to marry me and she had refused him. He had asked my mother at the suggestion of Tadashi, who had otherwise declined to talk about me because he too was in love with me.

So Kenji loved me, but what does it matter?

Not long after Tadashi and I were married I confessed to him that I didn't love him; I said spiteful, unforgivable things. Fortunately, though, after forty years it no longer matters. A dozen years back, when I could no longer live with all I had done and all that had been done to me, I wished for an end to my life. I wished it with all my heart, the way I had wished for Kenji and not for Tadashi, the way I had wished my mother dead, and the way I had as a young child wished for my dead father to live. But, then, my wish was not fulfilled, and when you live long enough, I've learned, so many wishes don't come true that one more doesn't make the difference. I am still here; in fact, I am even learning to dance. To celebrate Goro and Tomoe's twenty-fifth wedding anniversary, which is coming up next month, Tadashi has insisted that I learn. Every day at four o'clock he comes to my bed and pulls me up the same way Dr. Steiger once did, only he plays music. I can rumba, tango, even waltz when the mood suits me, and Tadashi, my husband of so many years, flatters me by saying I am not half bad. Following his lead, I bow and dip and spin around the room in a way that is both dizzying and ridiculous. I am you for an afternoon, light as a seventeen-year-old, and maybe for the first time without a thought in my head.

Come Fall

8
.
T o m o e

Everyone was asleep when the hospital called, but Melodie heard. Like me, she'd been waiting up all night, and when the phone on her bedstand rang she knew what it meant. She didn't answer it, let me take the news because it's my mother, instead she lay in her bed silently comforting me, letting me have my grief, which is the way it should be. Still, what's inevitable is hard to believe: they say Mama's life is over, but can death really put an end to so much life? Before going outside I have to spell it out for myself. "Baachan died at five twenty-seven." Then I add, "I'll be in the yard watering when you're ready to go." I stare at the words I've made for a minute, waiting for I don't know what, then I write Melodie's name on top and stick the white notepaper on the kitchen table next to her cereal and coffee so she'll see.

Gardening is a constant chore, and it's clear now that

Tadashi needs my help. Maybe he's getting old and losing his eyesight—he's always been so meticulous about the yard. Or maybe it's me. I haven't noticed as busy as I've been, but since Mama got bad the snails have taken over. I follow their raw, muddy trails on my hands and knees and then I spot them next to the bougainvillea bush, three huge ones grazing on my dichondra. Still in a crawl I watch them for a minute. Their slimy, gray antennae quiver and glisten in the morning shade and I would let them stay that way, half out of their shells, grotesque and unaware that I am watching them, except that that is not the way things work. Tadashi hasn't planted this garden for the last forty years to let it be eaten away by snails. One, two, three so that it will be painless I bring my fist down on their shells; then I hose down the driveway and pull some crabgrass.

I'm carrying a full bucket around back when I notice Melodie watching me from the brick steps that lead to the front door, out where all the neighbors can see her in her pink flannel nightgown. She's twenty years old, she'll graduate magna cum laude from college in spring, but this morning she may as well be a child. I have to look twice when I see her there. Out of the corner of my eye, without her knowing I am taking her in, I see the way she rubs her eye with one hand and waves at me with the other and it's enough to make me wonder if she hasn't been asleep all this time. Maybe she didn't hear the phone at all. Maybe it was me, by myself, silently taking in the news. I have a sudden mind to snatch the spade out of my bucket and hit her over the head with it, but I check myself. She is my daughter, and even if it has taken her this long to get out here, I am not without good sense.

I let her know what I'm thinking, though, because I do not look at her again. I look away where water from my driveway trails the gutter halfway to the next block. Then I unlatch the gate and tell her to go inside and get dressed.

When I was Melodie's age, I had a husband and a daughter, another one on the way. I never needed anyone to tell me what to do. But Melodie is different. I remember a comment Mama once made about my oldest. *Melodie's nature is buried in a deep place,* she said. She told me this along with a story about her own childhood in Japan. Mama grew up in Shimonoseki, a port on the southern tip of Honshu where her mother ran a fabric shop. Mama said that her family's store was the only one of its kind in Shimonoseki. For this reason it pulled in a good business and Mama never had to worry about money. But one day a customer whom she had seen in her mother's store pulled Mama aside on the street. *I am sorry for you,* he said.

Why? Mama had asked.

The man told her, *You have a face that does not yet know sadness.* Mama said she didn't think about this incident until years later, when she was harvesting grapes in California, pregnant with me. She thought about it then because she had married the man who had stopped her on the street that day and followed him to California in search of a better life.

My father taught Mama sadness even before his early death, but that is another story. I imagine that Mama saw in Melodie's hopeful smile an expression similar to the one she lost the day she left Japan—it is because my daughter has lived a sheltered life that I worry about her.

Inside smells warm like the coffee of any other morning. It's quiet with Tadashi already gone on his gardening route. Rio is asleep downstairs, Reiko sleeps above, and Goro sits at the kitchen table with the newspaper held up to his face. There's a sink full of dishes not far off, but no one except me notices that. Years ago Goro would have noticed. He'd say, "Here, let me help you with those, dear," but I have never liked anyone else doing my dishes. I wouldn't still have every dish I own intact from my wedding almost twenty-five years ago if I thought otherwise. I am proud to be able to say I've never chipped a dish, not a single one, though where Goro is concerned I am to blame for not doing things differently from the start. I was so happy back then to be living in this big blue house with its bay windows and fine furnishings. It did not seem like much to have Granny and Rio to care for. So what if I had to bring Granny her meals? I had to cook for Goro and myself, so how much of a problem could it have been to cook for one more? And with all the stories you hear about women not getting along with their in-laws, I never had that problem with Rio and Tadashi. Right from the start Rio welcomed me into this home. She told me things she'd never confided in anyone, and the way I'd been taught it was a privilege to know a person's heart, not a burden. I grew up poor, but my life had not taught me what it's like never to have enough, never to be satisfied, or shown me that goodness and pain could lie so close together in a person's heart. Twenty-five years ago when I hadn't a clue as to how Goro liked things, what I didn't know then is that he would have done anything to please me. He'd just been assigned to Bay Community Church the year we met, and if I had told him then that he belonged to me, not to the church, and that I was not marrying him to serve his grandmother, or his mother, he would have accepted that. But I can't complain. Twenty-five years ago we were as awkward as two new lovers are likely to be, and this morning when I woke him to tell him about Mama after the hospital called he held me there, webbed in sleep, and I could feel his heart beating in my ears as solid and loyal as when we first met.

"I'm back, Goro," I call to him from across the room, realizing from the way he flips the newspaper and belches that he thinks he's alone.

"Tomoe?" He puts the newspaper down. "Back from the hospital already?"

"No, dear, I've been outside watering."

"Oh?" He frowns. "Would you like me to go with you then, to the hospital?"

"No, Melodie is coming with me."

"All right, then," he says. "You're all right, then?"

"Yes." I pause. "You have some time this morning, before you leave the house?"

"Yes. You'd like me to come with you?"

"No." For the first time in I don't know how long I don't know what I want. Once I wanted a big house with bay windows, then a job that would take me out of that house. I wanted children who would grow to be independent, but now I have no one but myself to turn to. "Maybe if you could do the dishes while we're gone."

"The dishes?" He says this as if I'm joking.

"Yes, since we had better get going. We probably should have left already. Melodie!" I call down the hall.

"Of course I'll wash them right now."

Melodie runs into the kitchen dangling a pair of tennis shoes by the laces. "Good morning, Daddy." She strides to the table wearing the same pair of jeans she's had on since she arrived home and greets her father with a kiss.

"Did you bring anything to wear to the funeral?" I ask.

She raises a hand to her mouth. "I didn't think of that."

I have a black suit, I think to myself, *but I'll be wearing it.* "Take my charge card then and buy yourself something nice."

"Don't worry, Mom, I'll take care of it later."

"Don't argue with me. And you'd better go right away because there'll be enough to do later on."

"But the stores aren't open yet."

"You know what I mean."

As Melodie and I drive east toward the hospital, the morning sky gives me a lonely feeling. Maybe it's because of my childhood that I get sad in fall. Maybe it's because autumn always brought back the end of harvest and come fall the hired workers would leave my family to face the bleak winter alone. Or maybe it's the same for everyone, maybe fall is just a lonely season. "What's your favorite season?" I wonder, turning to Melodie.

"Fall," she says, without having to think. "It's beautiful, isn't it."

"It is beautiful," I tell her.

"Besides, October's my birthday month. What's your favorite season?"

I think for a minute, and then I know that it would have to be summer. "When I was growing up, times were always good in summer," I tell Melodie. "Around harvest season people would come from all over to help out. There'd be lots to do and plenty to eat."

Melodie leans her head back and closes her eyes. Through the years she's asked me questions about my childhood, but I wasn't born with a good memory like my daughter's. Melodie can tell you all about her first day of school: what she wore, what I packed in her Cinderella lunch box. (She tells me I reminded her three times not to break her thermos.) She can remember the names of her classmates in the first grade and the word for which she won the third grade spelling bee. *Infallible,* I think it was. She even knew what it meant. The thing that marked my childhood was seasons—the color of dust hanging in the autumn sky and harsh winters followed by springs when I'd climb the fattest tree I could find and eat cherries until my stomach cramped. Other than that, I don't remember much.

The hospital has become like home in the week since Mama was admitted; I've driven here at all hours of the morning and night, eaten, slept, and prayed here. I know the click of my own heels against the linoleum floors, the right button to push in the elevator, the names of all the fourth-floor nurses and just how each one treats Mama. Only this morning there is no trace of Mama anywhere. When I arrive at her room the slippers on which I'd marked KANEMORI in black letters are missing, even Mama's bed is gone. Melodie and I eye the empty space from the doorway until Mrs. Hansen, Mama's roommate, turns her head and begins wiggling her fingers for us to come. Melodie does not take a direct path to her bedside. I watch from the doorway as she walks around the place where Mama's bed had been; then I follow her. She stands respectfully to my side, and I put my ear down close because

Mrs. Hansen has lung cancer and can speak only in a raspy whisper. "Terrible," she says.

The pungent smell of her breath makes me draw my face back, but I take her hand and she closes her fingers around mine.

"Terrible," she mouths again.

I want to ask what is so terrible, but I'm scared of her breath, of what she might say, of all that I know without needing to ask. I need to let go, to do what I am here to do, but I am not able to move just yet.

"Terrible, terrible, terrible," until her eyelids drop, her grip relaxes, her breathing slows with sleep.

Looking down at Mrs. Hansen's shell of a body, I wonder how she continues to survive and I pity her. Since Mama was admitted a week ago, Mrs. Hansen has had only one visitor. A son, I think. Mama was lucky to have raised daughters. Because she has daughters, there has always been someone there with her.

Melodie has jotted down directions to the morgue, but getting there is a complicated process. I have lost count of the hallways; certain I've made a wrong turn, I am about to tell Melodie we'd better retrace our steps when a familiar voice booms down the hall. "Enough." There is no mistaking the urgency in my oldest sister's voice. "ENOUGH."

We walk through the next set of swinging doors and the morgue is there, and in it my sisters Miwa and Patti, the youngest, facing off at each other. "I told you I'll take care of it." Miwa lowers her voice when she sees me. "You're here, Tomoe," she greets me.

"What's the problem?" I ask.

"No problem," says Miwa.

"Miwa wants to sew Mama a suit," Patti protests.

They have been planning the funeral, arguing over what Mama should wear, and I want to say, *What have they done with her body? Where is she?* but Miwa is the oldest, and I know better than to interrupt her when she's mad. Besides, she's fierce. Miwa and Patti both flew in from out of town, but Miwa was the only one brave enough to stay at Mama's house this past week. Patti was afraid that if Mama died during the night her ghost would visit and she wouldn't know what to say. Miwa, being Buddhist, also believes that the ghost of the deceased returns to its home immediately after death, only she's never been at a loss for things to say. When I was a child, Miwa was the one who issued me orders. Every day she'd wake me up with a list of chores, and I'd go through the day afraid that my mother would die if I didn't do everything exactly as she'd said.

"You don't have to go to the trouble, Miwa." I cannot tell whether Patti is trying to be helpful, or whether she just wants to get her way. "I'll run over to Neiman Marcus and buy her a great suit," she says.

"I've got it under control, Tomoe." Miwa winks at me with both eyes as if to say, you are with me on this one.

She is the oldest, and years ago Patti would not have dreamed of defying her. Standing here in the morgue, a measuring tape strung around her neck, Miwa could be an undertaker. But she is still my oldest sister, and I notice for the first time how she has aged. The skin on her neck sags, and the bosom my sisters and I always admired has sunken. "Hi, Melodie," she says, suddenly noticing my daughter.

"Hi, Auntie Miwa," Melodie says. "You look so tired."

Evidently Miwa spent last night taking stock of things, then trying to find the suit she'd sewn Mama for last New Year's. Wanting to be prepared for the funeral, she'd spent the night wondering where the suit had gone. I remember it—all hand-stitched in gray, the only color Mama wore. Mama gave me the suit Miwa had sent her, the way she gave away every gift she'd ever received. In her younger days she'd go out shopping after work, then stack things in my car on weekends when I'd visit. Later, when she couldn't make it to the store, she'd offer me gifts people had given her. Mama supplied me with dish towels, sheets, socks, even underwear; it was no use arguing with her when she wanted to give you something. But I could never tell Miwa how Mama forced me to take that suit. Now Miwa, measuring tape around her neck, seems determined to give Mama something she can't give away.

"Patti," I speak sternly to my youngest sister, "there are other things for you to do. Arrangements will have to be made at the funeral home. Have you called them yet?"

"Yes, they just left with Mama's body."

"Why did you let them take her before I got here?"

Patti looks at me blankly.

"They couldn't wait," Miwa says.

"Why did you take so long to get ready?" I ask Melodie.

"You didn't need to see her," Miwa says. Suddenly I am glad I didn't give the suit Miwa sewed for Mama to the Salvation Army. When Miwa leaves I will send her that suit by airmail.

I spend an hour at the hospital composing a list of funeral preparations with Miwa, Patti, and Melodie, until it's time to go to work. I take my credit cards from my wallet and hold them out to Melodie. "Don't forget to buy a dress."

Melodie tries to push my arm away, but I am stronger than she is. Before I leave she says, "You don't have to go to work today, Mom."

"I know that," I tell her, and I leave.

I have tried to teach both my daughters how important it is to do what you can for people while they're alive. I knew I didn't have to come to work, but what's the point in hanging around the hospital now that Mama is dead? *It's no use*, I think to myself as I schedule last-minute summer flights, honeymoons, business trips, Melodie's flight back to Los Angeles and Miwa's to Stockton.

I have worked at Stern Travel for a dozen years, over

which time I have booked thousands of flights, hundreds as favors for my family, and yet I have never gone anywhere. *I have never gone anywhere—Mama is dead;* these two thoughts fall against each other like playing cards. I jot numbers on flight vouchers: 87, Mama's age; 5:27, the time of death; 10/28, the date. I note these numbers in black ink like a formula to account for my loss. As if death can be accounted for, I count the things that remain: my daughter Melodie, but she is leaving; Nomi, my youngest, is gone to Japan and who knows if she will receive my telegram in time to come back. All my life I have cared for others—my younger sisters Emi-chan, Keiko, Shidzue, Mieko, Hana, and Patti, and then my two children. When they left I had Mama. Then I consider my husband and a perverse thought crosses my mind. *When I get home tonight I will dress him in diapers and feed him like I have fed Mama.* The bright morning sunshine has dissolved the lettering on my computer screen to black, or maybe I've gone blind.

Maybe because she notices that my pace has come to a halt for the first time in a dozen years, my boss offers her condolences. "Just think, I lost my mother last year," she says.

"I know." Her insincerity makes me smile. In all the years I've worked with her has she ever once mentioned her mother?

I want to say, *My loss is not like yours, you don't understand.* Losing Mama is not only losing a mother; Miwa took care of me and I raised the younger ones. There were eight of us all together, all girls, and we looked after one another because for as far back as any of us could remember Mama had too many children and not enough time. Before it was even light out she'd be working the fields. She'd work from before it got light until after dark. She worked until her body no longer functioned, until it seemed that the older she got the younger she became, until she stopped working altogether and became my child.

I remember going to visit Mama late one afternoon and finding her seated on the floor in the middle of the room. I had come in from the sunlight and the entire room lay hidden in shadows, but I called out from the doorway, "Mama, nani o shiyo?" *Is that you there?*

When she didn't respond, only sat perfectly still, I thought for a moment that her spirit had departed. Next to her, green chrysanthemum stalks, tall and hideously bald, crowned the rim of a bucket, and all around white petals lay scattered, plucked like feathers from a chicken.

"Aren't those the chrysanthemums Patti sent you?"

"I've been gardening."

Separated from the main room by a waist-high counter, I thought to myself, *Best to go on as usual.* I picked a roll of toilet paper and a dish sponge off the top of the brown paper bag I'd carried in, and wondering, *Why do old people all get this way?* I pulled out the buckwheat noodles I had brought for her dinner.

As I waited for the water to boil I listened to the faucet drip *plink, plink,* I refused to look at her in the other room sitting beside those naked flowers. The soba frothed and tumbled in the boiling water, and I called out the same simple questions I asked her every day, *How are you? What have you been doing today?* Usually she'd tell me she was fine, list the things she'd done since morning, but that afternoon her voice came out in a low rumble. The only word I could make out was *nigai.* "Bitter" was the answer to every question. I remember thinking to myself, *They get like this when they're old. What a pity it is to live past your usefulness.*

"Everyone here is nigai," Mama repeated. "I can taste it."

"Who's nigai? People can't be nigai."

"No, everyone is nigai. I hear them say to each other that I am a slob. They laugh at me."

"Who laughs at you? You tell me who and I'll go talk to them."

"It's in the walls. This place is nigai."

"Uso tsuki," I told her. "You're making up lies."

"No," Mama retorted. "Why should I lie?"

What could I say to that? I set a bowl of steaming soba on the placemat in front of her, but she remained still, head lowered, palms folded in her lap. The tip of her chin quivered in a way that spoke of both anger and fear and it scared me to see her that way. "Doesn't the soba look delicious?" I asked.

"Sooo neh," she said, same as always. "It looks delicious."

I watched her hands tremble as she brought the

ohashi to her mouth. *When you get old your hands don't work anymore.* After a long pause, she laid the chopsticks on the placemat and gazed down at her lap. *Your legs won't do what you tell them to do. You have to be firm with them. Better not to be old.* Then she looked up and it was as if she was seeing me for the first time. "Tomoe, neh," she said. "Listen here. When I come back, I'm going to be a beautiful young girl. You'll be proud of me then." She clasped her hands together and bowed her head from me to the Obutsudan where fresh sasaki sprigs and a red apple shined for Buddha.

I removed the ohashi from Mama's bowl and placed a fork in her hand. "A fork is easier. You must eat now."

After lunch I unpinned her hair for a shampoo. The silver strands dipped well below her shoulders, almost to the waist, and I brushed them, the way I'd done for both my daughters, until they shone. The hair was thinning though, and her scalp showed through and smelled of hair oil, and of decay. I looked down at the blouse she was wearing, the same gray one she'd had for years, and her slacks, threadbare and patched at the knees. "No wonder people talk," I told her. "You have a closet full of clothes and look how you dress."

"Nigai." She was mad at the world.

"Don't talk like that," I scolded. At that moment, with her shoulders slumped and the odor of her hair strong on my hands, she seemed vulnerable in a way I'd never thought she could be and I was sad for her. Still, I had to be firm so that she wouldn't get too full of self-pity. "You know it's true."

"What is in your heart is most important," she reminded me.

"Yes," I told her, "but in this world appearances are important too."

I gave her hair a good washing and watched on as she scrubbed herself clean. The water gurgled and steam rose, and that afternoon, standing over the tub, I realized how her life had changed forever. Without my knowing it, time had come for her. In great numbers the years had carried her away to a place where now she needed me. She sat there in the tub, close enough that I could bolster her if she slipped, but where was this place she now occupied, so far away from me? My mother, whom I had always known and yet couldn't remember from my childhood, who had maybe never been a child herself, needed me to feel safe in this new world. And yet she was a stranger to me. And what I felt then was neither good nor bad. It was just an observation of life that flashed through my head, maybe as a result of standing still. And maybe she read my mind, because before I left that afternoon she said to me, "You have done so much for me, but I have never been much of a mother to you. What will I ever do to repay you?"

■　■　■

Like me, my sisters must have known Mama's life would not go on forever, only it wasn't until this last week that Miwa and Patti arrived. Mama's first night in the hospital the doctor said she was on the verge of coma, but when Miwa spoke to her she opened her eyes. By midweek the doctor had prescribed Dilaudid. Then Mama began dreaming out loud. She spent a whole afternoon talking to herself in a dialect of Japanese I don't understand. She must have gone back to her childhood. And that night Mama's whole body shook as if under the weight of a full sack of rice and every muscle in her face became tense. *It's so heavy*, she kept saying. I didn't know what to do, but Miwa had a good suggestion. *Put some of it down*, she said. Almost immediately Mama's body relaxed. *Ah, that's much better*, she sighed. Later in the night huge tears drained from Mama's eyes and she complained about onions. Miwa still remembers how she used to help Mama peel crate after crate of onions to cook for the harvest workers. But that night Mama directed her orders at me. *Tomoe*, she called, *please help me*. From my position at her bedside I took Mama's hand. What else could I do? Her eyes summoned me with all the fierceness of a child.

"Tomoe, help me," she said.

My sisters had said their good-byes, but when it came time for me to speak I had nothing to say. Mama and I had said everything we needed to say to each other through the years; now I wanted her to die. And yet how could I let her go? *Mama*, I called again, and she squeezed my hand.

Yesterday afternoon it was Miwa who forced me to go home. When Mama clenched her teeth in pain and I rose to comfort her, Miwa pulled me back. "You must let her die."

"She is dying."

"No, Tomoe, Mama will not die as long as you keep calling her back."

I dream of death. Mama is a young woman planting seeds in a hot, arid field, and I am a child again watching her work through the cracks of a wicker basket. Before me the earth splits open like the bed of a waterless creek. Flies swarm around me. They land on my ears, in my hair, on my tongue, and I'm afraid they'll get inside me. I raise my arms to swat them, but I can't catch any. Then Mama's large, calloused hand pinches one out of the air. She holds it by the wings and bends over me blocking the sun with her large, shadowy body until her face is only inches away from mine. It is the face I have always known, but it is not Mama's. She takes a breast from her blouse and holds my head up for me to drink, but there is no nipple there, just saggy, puckered flesh, and I wake up in a panic. "She's dead," I say to the darkness, and beside me Goro's breath is rhythmic and slow.

■　■　■

I've set the funeral off more days than I should and this has upset Patti, who says she's already been away way too long. I tell everyone the date I've arranged is the only one that will work out for everyone, but secretly I've made the delay for myself. Everyone should be here, and it's only right that you should have enough time to come home. I don't ask much of my children, but even though you are in Tokyo and I am here in San Francisco, Mama is, after all, my mother and hopefully I have taught my children to do what is right.

The five days that lead up to the funeral are filled with waiting. I try to keep the house neat for friends who stop by to offer condolences, but other than tidying up there isn't much to do. Your name comes up more than once—strangers and family alike wanting to know "how is she?" (meaning "where are you?") It's enough to drive me crazy. Each time the phone rings my heart rises, then sinks again when it is not you, and meanwhile the only thought running through my head is how far away Tokyo is. *Tokyo is so far away*, and I try to let my mind wander there, over ocean, through crowded streets and parks decorated with autumn foliage to the room you have written me about lined with knickknacks and souvenirs, just like your room at home. But how can I imagine you there, in a place I've never been? Each day I only think how far away Tokyo is until the morning of the funeral comes at last and I awaken with the feeling that you are dead. I have tried to reach you; I raised you with my own hands and taught you everything in my heart worth knowing. I have given you all the love I have to give, but you are gone and you are not coming back. It is all I can do to remind myself that today i will bury Mama.

I dress in black, and in me there is blackness. Now I let the coarse black wool rub against smooth black silk, and the black of stockings, slip, blouse, skirt blend with the black of my hair and the black in my heart because I mourn not my mother, but my daughter. Mama's friends and family file into the temple in a single line and fill the pews with a blackness that makes me indistinguishable from the others. *Didn't I once wish for my children to find security in appearances?* Who but me knows what lies beneath the layers I wear and threatens to seep out into the air like poison.

The priest, an older Nihonzin, introduces himself to me before the service and I wonder if he can see my heart. He holds my hands between his, and I look directly into his eyes defying him to scent my heart's odor, but his words tell me that he is immune to poison. He tells me only that my mother was a kind woman; then he chants something in Japanese I can't understand and drifts away. And that is how the service progresses. The priest reciting or chanting, and my not understanding. You might recognize these words, definitely Mama would, but I am alone. I am ashamed of the blackness in my heart and of the space to my right where you should sit. To my left is Melodie. Our shoulders touch, she is that close, but the other space, the one to my right where you should be, is empty.

Sandalwood incense is lit; from the altar near the pulpit it drifts down in a smoky thread, straight up my nostrils, both calling me into the room and threatening to suffocate me. There is the heavy smell of incense and along with it the sweetness of flowers everywhere that start my eyes watering. My nose begins to burn and it is all I can do to swallow. I hold my breath. I wonder how I will make it through the service without choking or, worse yet, suffocating, but now that it has begun I have no choice.

"Nigai," I whisper to myself.

"What, Mom?" Melodie bends over, touches my shoulder.

"Nothing," I say, but to myself again, nigai. It repeats itself loudly and to no one in particular though the image taking root is Mama. Late afternoon shadows fill the room where she sits amidst tall, bald stalks of chrysanthemum; Mama hunched over a bucket ripping the white petals off one by one. I bet she smelled death hovering around her that afternoon and cutting the petals was the only way she could find to release life back into the air.

Now, with you gone, I don't know how I can hold death back. I look down at my hands, chafed by water and air and life. Gar-dee-nee-a, I once taught you, my baby. I plucked one from Tadashi's garden and held it under your nose so that you could sniff its perfume. And in the spring, chrysanthemums; wild roses in the summer. You could find each one with your eyes closed. Now the smell has turned nigai and the flowers lining each pew shed their bitter colors for me to see. They bleed together, shaped into wreaths, hearts, and pillows, and I am imagining you, drifting over miles of salt water and wind when a familiar voice calls out in front of me—the priest chanting again. There is something powerful, life sustaining in the sounds he makes through the black hollow of his throat and nostrils. He held my hands together and I believed he did not understand, but his words wash over me until I recognize in them something as familiar as the sound of loneliness.

A man clears his throat and swallows hard; it is Tadashi. "Granny, quiet now!" he strains to whisper. In the room that contains us all, Rio sits next to him breathing a sigh that is closer to a hum.

"Tomoe, I can't— Help me," Granny pleads.

"Granny, quiet, I said," Tadashi repeats. I turn around to quiet her myself, only before I can speak I realize her behavior is not out of place. She is chanting with the priest, following right along with him: *Namu amida butsu*, they say. *Namu amida butsu*.

The room falls silent. With closed eyes the priest is my father. He bows his head low and holds his hands out to Mama with a kind of reverence I never saw him summon while she was alive. Now that she is dead, unable to see him there, palms outstretched to her—I see.

Miwa was right to pull me back from Mama's bedside. I knew it was her time, but I called to her because I did not want to be left. I wanted her to stay as long as she would because I needed a mother and I did not know what I would do without her. Late in the afternoon, Mama's body curved around a bucket of dying chrysanthemums, she said she wanted to repay me, and all I wanted was for her to keep living.

I treated her in the best way a daughter can treat a mother until there was nothing more to be done. I have no regrets.

A procession of mourners forms around me. Mrs. Shimbashi clutches a cane with one hand to support her weight and with the other she grasps my hand. I do not recognize her at first, but the smell of mothballs hangs heavy around her and I remember how Mrs. Shimbashi gave Mama warm clothes for all of us to wear the first winter in camp when we had nothing—that same smell emanated from everything she gave us. There is the child-less widow whom Mama used to bring by the apartment after my father died, when she worked at Tenri restaurant; her neighbors from Alameda Street; and strangers come too. They pass with their heads bowed, some more quickly than others, until their faces bob and swim like hungry fish.

Or maybe it is me alone gasping for breath when Tadashi approaches. "I'm sorry, Tomoe," he says. I take his hand and feel how solid it is, how it reaches down into my darkness like a stone. Reiko is on his arm. This is the first time she's been seen in public for years, and she eyes her strange surroundings with the carefulness and wonder of a child set loose at the zoo.

"Otearai," she whispers to Melodie, as she passes, I have to go to the bathroom. Then to me, "Where's Nomi?"

"She's not here, Granny," Tadashi says.

"I know that."

"She's in Tokyo, remember?"

"Where?"

"Tokyo," I almost shout.

"Ah," Reiko nods, "that's right."

"Come on." Tadashi tries to move her along, but Granny refuses to budge. A tear is pooling in the corner of her eye and she stands directly in front of me, staring intently. "Nomi is with my mother now," she says.

And I am about to say, no, Granny, Nomi is in Tokyo, your mother is dead, but I stop myself.

"Come on, Granny," Tadashi insists.

"Otearai . . ." she chants as she moves away, and I tap Melodie's shoulder. "Take her, would you?"

Melodie scoots off and the last one in line is Rio. Tadashi has moved on with Reiko and she approaches alone, unsteady on her feet as if being pulled in every direction but forward. "Tomoe," she calls to me.

"Yes." She is my burden, and I watch her come closer

until she is standing with all her sadness and pallor in front of me.

"I'm sorry." She takes my hand. I know she is sincere, but I am not moved by her sorrow.

"It's too bad Nomi isn't here," she sighs at last.

"Yes." I want to defend you, and yet Rio is maybe the only one besides me who understands. A tear wells in my eye, the first since Mama died. I know Rio loves me, and I know she loves you. You are the bridge between us—her blood mixed with mine, and without you here, I am left stupidly holding her hand. It is not enough.

Airfields

9

Nomi

I think of you all the time, and always I am back in Japan.
I am in a cafe sipping a peach-flavored milkshake, or lying
naked on my back watching my stomach rise and fall. You
appear through the rim of my glass, over the peak of my
belly, a darker image of myself. Distorted, protracted, you
envelop me as the night progresses and become almost
invisible by morning, though just when I am dreaming
you gone I awaken. For seven years I have not spoken to
anyone about you. You have lain dormant until now, I am
no longer certain of our connection, only of my need to
preserve you, or to release myself because I no longer
know what is real.

Because of you, I am reaching back further than I ever
thought my mind would take me. Where endings are concerned there is no hope. I never remember how books
end, or lives. I have no memory for sadness. I need to feel

sweat dripping down my face and between my breasts to be reminded of hot summers in Japan and of the distance I've traveled. But now I think that if I can find a beginning, then I can go on. If I can find a beginning I will know where to go. Sometimes I think it is you. But I am not the beginning and so it cannot be you.

The truth lies somewhere with Grandma Rio, the day she tried to end her life. I was seven then, and I am twenty-seven now, and that day repeats as if no time has passed from then till now. I want to know why memory works that way. Why time stops when the heart runs into something it can't pump through. I am not a child anymore, but I need to know why that night when I could not sleep, when I was sure that my life depended on one word, on bringing to class the next day a foreign word that I could not think of on my own, my grandmother lay contemplating an end to her life. In the morning my mother's car would not start and I knew that meant something was wrong, but I didn't yet know what it meant to be late for school. I was puzzling over "tardy" because I could not fathom "death." I was scared to leave my mother, unaware that my grandmother had already deserted me. I was trying to save my life when my grandmother was trying to end hers. But the truth is that my heart has never understood the difference between late and absent, leaving and being left.

The heart distends time; in the heart time is stretched,

stopped, and cut short, but I did not understand then what I know now. Every day, as an act of faith, when I went downstairs to visit with my grandmother, I listed off the events of my day because I was trying to protect her. I told her stories about the pet rabbit who lived in the schoolyard in a cage, the cow that was once brought in from a dairy to show how milk is made, the neon fish my teacher kept in the classroom under fluorescent light. I was the magician who could pull a rabbit, a cow, a fish from my hat and make my grandmother's ribs dance with laughter. Like a magician I performed my tricks to delight and amuse, and maybe for a short time I was successful, but how long can a seven-year-old be expected to sustain a magic act? And how well without any assistance? I could have used some help from my mother, who had her hands full, or my father, who isn't part of my memory.

My father was minister of the church where my sister and I went on Sundays. Church was the place my mother took us to be with him, the man who stood high on his pulpit telling us all to close our eyes and pray. My father asked us all to believe in God's will, but he was not there when Grandma Rio made her choice clear. When she decided that her will was better than God's and my mother's face could no longer hide disbelief, then the eyes of the church opened outward, not on my father, but on us, his family.

Years later, my father decided he had been wrong

about God, but he did not see what I had sensed all along:
God had not forsaken my father; my father had betrayed
his family. His betrayal fumed and broiled inside me along
with the childish hope that he, not God, could save us if
he wanted to. But it wasn't until after my father lost his
faith that he appeared in my life, and by that time I was
growing up with an agenda of my own on which he had
no place. I did not want to bear witness to his fall from
faith. When God had been the focus of his life he had left
me alone, and at one time maybe I had resented it, but
then I had grown accustomed to life without a father, and
at fifteen his sudden interest in me felt unnatural, unholy
even, and with his attention began a series of never-end-
ing nightmares. Of the field where I burned ants under a
magnifying lens, and I am dancing toward fuming smoke-
stacks not far off, or inside the church running to escape a
maze from which I have never broken free. Inside the
church, birds become hornets and live rabbits are buried
beneath the lawn where children play. These dreams are
gaps in my memory, forever playing themselves out. I
know this now. They are as familiar to me as the memories of my own childhood, but the gaps are parts of myself
that don't belong to me.

My father, nullifier of dreams, bade me good-bye the
night before I was to leave for college with an offhand
remark that San Francisco is the place people come to find

their dreams. His demeanor remained unchanged as he added that the suicide rate is higher here than anywhere else in the world. After all, people are no more likely to find their dreams here than where they came from, and when they realize this they remember the bridge that brought them west and take their final imaginative leap from fantasy into the cold salt waters of death. It was late at night and he stood shadowed outside my door while I was packing and told me this with no apparent context, instead of good-bye, and without a trace of sadness. He still chooses to ignore the importance of place in determining destiny. He will not bow to the strength of the human will or believe in the potency of desire; he prefers instead to place his trust in statistics. But I was not about to give up my life. I'd seen my grandmother and mother give theirs up to depression and a family that couldn't appreciate them. I wanted no more of that history and I was bent on proving my father wrong.

The next day, a mildly sunny afternoon in September, I drove across the Bay Bridge from San Francisco into Berkeley with my mind set on a new life. I'd done this many times before, crossed over the water with the windows down, music blaring, hair strewn out behind me like tail feathers, only this time I would not be returning.

Tasha had been the first friend I made at school. She walked with me along Telegraph Avenue and introduced me to her secrets over dinner at Sargenti's. She talked about Egypt, Africa, Israel, and men, and like a lover, she filled my mouth with exotic new tastes. Everything about Tasha was large, bigger than me, more voluptuous, and new. Her teeth, her laughter, her flaming red hair. It wasn't that I lacked height, and I was gaining color in my own way; it was that I wanted to trade histories with Tasha, hand off my past to her and commit her travels as my own into memory. And if such a switch resulted in the physical appearance of suntanned dismissiveness that would be fine with me. And so when she told me I was a lot like her, it was not pride I felt, but utter hopefulness that the world might split open for me the way it appeared to have done for her, just wide enough to let me in, to allow me some of its pleasures.

After Tasha had divulged her life story to me, I told her about my dream of Japan, and she nodded as I talked and told me to go for it.

"You and I are a lot alike," she told me, popping an ice cube into her mouth and cracking it between her molars. "We won't stop short of our goals, and no one's going to get in our way, right?"

Tasha had ordered for me, we'd eaten, the bitterness of coffee was dissolving into icy water, and I was savoring the taste of an incredibly rich dessert. "Right," I said, though I wasn't sure what she was talking about.

Then she gasped. "Don't look over your shoulder but the T.A. I met in Geology 111 whom I've been swooning

over for weeks just walked in the door alone and— Oh
my God, oh my God . . ."

I watched Tasha's face as the freckles on her cheeks
began to dance and her hazel eyes turned a bright green.
The T.A. slid a chair over to our table and Tasha introduced him as Porter, and suddenly everything was movement. The clatter of a fork falling to the floor, and candles
which had been lit now reflected gold in every direction.

That night, as if in a dream, my love for Tasha was
transformed. I was nineteen years old and had never tasted
zabaione or felt unbound by gravity in a public place
when a hand brushed against my leg. Tasha's eyes said,
pay attention and you will learn something. But below the
table Porter's hand moving along my thigh made me pay
attention to him, and all but that sensation was lost to me.

His apartment overlooked the East Bay and rather than
have our privacy disturbed by my roommate, I took the
train out to see him. He picked me up on his moped and
as soon as we were locked away in his flat, the sex happened almost immediately, with my back pressed against
the front door, on the kitchen table, the toilet seat, and
then one night on the third-floor balcony while I stood
watching the moon rise over the water. That night, as I
clutched the metal railing, the water below me crested in
tiny quarter-moon arcs, which grew like a message racing
for shore.

"Tell me you love me," Porter mouthed in my ear, as he pressed his chest against my back.

"Okay," I said, "I love you."

"Say it like you mean it," he whispered.

"I love you, I mean it," I growled.

The moon continued to rise and the slightest hint of salt air blew in off the water. Porter reached up under my shirt and cupped my breasts, moving his hands slowly, barely touching my skin and I had half an urge to tell him to stop it, but it felt good to be standing there, watching the water lull into shore, and a moan escaped from my throat, or maybe it was a seagull far off, hovering.

Porter's hands slid away from my breasts. Unzipping my jeans he moved his hands over my belly down to my crotch and my moans began coming more steadily, frightening me a little, standing almost exposed, with the lights from nearby apartments flicking on now like not so distant stars. Then he slid my pants down around my ankles and began moving inside me with his arms still encircling me, hands exploring my body in the moonlight, and me responding with movements of my own that seemed shameless there on the balcony, with the sound of cars passing on the street behind us, and I knew that my moaning could be heard by anyone listening but no longer cared because all that concerned me now was the unbearable longing I felt, desire that would not be sated until it had been undone somewhere down deep, and it burned in my womb, down my legs, spreading out to my arms and fingertips, and I could feel the heat of my body penetrating the coldness of the railing, taste traces of metal alchemized by the sweat of my palms, and hear Porter behind me as he whispered again in my ear, "Tell me you love me."

I did not respond right away. I don't know how long after that I continued to move with him, made speechless by my own passion. The words began repeating themselves back as soon as he had mouthed them and I had wanted to spit them out at once, but instead they remained inside my head and my lips were sealed, head thrown back against his chest. Maybe I knew I would be changed by these words, or that the change in me had already taken place, but I could not stop holding off what I had been holding back for so long, savoring the sweat trapped between our bodies, him thrusting against me now in short, quick strokes, my moan a continuous wail, until in the moment before my climax I conjured you out of the connection that was now taking shape between Porter and me, and you were formed there on the third-floor landing that night, forged out of intimacy, longing, and leaving, a yet shapeless image of what was to come.

In the morning when I awoke in Porter's bed, the color of the sky outside his bedroom window reminded me of the lining of an abalone shell. I was six the first time I saw one, hard and crusty on the outside, then the soft, magnificent inside that was mine when my mother had scraped off the meat.

The quarter-mooned blackness of the night before had been the shaping of our history. With him I didn't think about Japan, couldn't think about leaving, even though I had long been on my way. In the airport terminal I made my way down a corridor with red-carpeted walls into the shell of the plane that would take me to Japan, alone.

There were tears, I am sure, on the way from SFX to Haneda. There was the stopover in Hawaii and my clumsy fingers dialing back to Porter's apartment on the East Bay. Dialing and forgetting, then remembering again, then hanging up the receiver. In a dream I am trying to reach him. I have something urgent to tell him and I am trying to get through but my fingers cannot remember. My fingers never remember, but I refuse to hang up until it is morning. My eyes open to sunlight and I believe, then, that the dream is over.

I stayed in Kyoto from August until the end of September, with a childless old couple. I see them as the train approaches, standing a safe distance back on the platform, watching for me. Her hair curls stiffly around her face, defiant of the thick summer air. She wears a brown skirt and a white long-sleeved blouse and her husband stands next to her. He is dressed in blue, a wool suit, in the middle of summer, the only one he owns? They look out of place there, in the middle of August, and I know with out a doubt that they are waiting for me, that they have been waiting a very long time, and my heart sinks. I have come all this way not to have to care about family, only to find them and their sweaty faces full of worry. They are pitiful, really, and I do not need more parents. The train has stopped and I do not want to debark, but because I must, I want to walk past them, pretend I am someone else. It is not me they are waiting for. I am just another black-haired, brown-eyed, Japanese person with some place to get to in a hurry. I make believe I know where I am going; I am walking past them into my own life when my journey is curtailed. I hear my name and I am defense-less to resist. Smelling like shoyu and fried fish, Mrs. Yamashita loops her arm around mine and it takes less than a second for the Japan of my imagination to disap-pear. There is talk of dinner, which she has spent days preparing, and what do I think of this unbearable summer heat? She tells me that she and Mr. Yamashita have no children and now here I am and I wonder if there is a word in Japanese for destiny.

On a rainy morning at the end of September I took a train to Nishi-o-tesugi to get away from them and when I ar-rived back late they were standing there, just like that first day in August, only it was dark. It was cold, they were wet and huddled with worried faces under their umbrella, and I could not bear to see them that way, or understand why they would stand waiting for me in the rain, unless, as I imagined, they'd guessed my secret. I was three months pregnant by then, forever tired, irritable, and queasy. Though they had never seen me any other way, I saw in their eyes the full weight of my disgrace. I was shamed by a past they would never know, and afraid too that the impossible would happen, that somehow the news of my pregnancy would leak back to my mother in San Francisco. The Yamashitas didn't have a phone, could not have spoken enough English to say, let alone write, the word "pregnant"; still, my secret reduced the thousands of miles of ocean separating Kyoto from San Francisco to the space of a single word, and the thought that my mother might hear my secret shut my mind and body down in defeat.

And so the leaving began again. Leaving to save my life like a convict fleeing from the scene of her crime, but sloppily because I left behind a track of lies that would follow me to Tokyo. I told the old couple that I had gotten a job in Tokyo, and my mother that the Yamashitas could not afford to have me stay anymore, and that the only other place for me was in Tokyo. She might have seen through this, but if she did she said nothing.

In Tokyo I rented a four-and-a-half-tatami-mat room,

and from my room I wrote letters home. To Grandma Rio I told how expensive books were, so costly that I could not afford to buy any. She sent back Freud's *Civilization and Its Discontents*, Nietzche's *Beyond Good and Evil*, and Sylvia Plath's *Bell Jar* and *Colossus*. It was not strange for her to do this when I considered that the first book I ever received had been from her—a leather-bound copy of *Leaves of Grass* when I turned six. She subscribed me to *Scientific American* for my tenth birthday and *Mother Jones* when I went off to college. For my twentieth birthday in Tokyo she sent me a box of chocolates that arrived two weeks late, stale and broken. Having sat brooding that my birthday had passed for the first time ever uncelebrated, I chose to interpret those chocolates, the only gift I received that year, as a sign. Hopeful that their message might be revealed to me, I placed them in the middle of my kotatsu table, sat myself ceremoniously in front of them, and devoured each broken bit without interruption. Hours later, full of disgust for what I had done, I licked my fingers clean, and wrote a note to my grandmother:

> *Thanks for the chocolates, they were exactly what I'd been wanting and I ate them all. Also, I've been reading the Plath poems and my favorite is "Metaphors": I'm a riddle in nine syllables, / An elephant, a ponderous house, / A melon strolling on two tendrils. / O red fruit, ivory, fine timbers! / This loaf's big with its yeasty rising. / Money's new-minted*

*in this fat purse. / I'm a means, a stage, a cow in a calf. /
I've eaten a bag of green apples, / Boarded the train there's no
getting off.*

How much more explicit could I have been? It might
have been insanity, but I am speaking candidly when I say
that I could not distinguish between my grandmother's
gift of chocolates, Plath's "Metaphors," and my own pregnancy, that I was attempting to give my secret away in my
coded silence. If she looked carefully, she would have seen
"help me" planted between each word, but by that time I
had entered my fourth month of pregnancy, too far away
and ignoble to be rescued. Still, I chose my words to my
grandmother as carefully as I could. I did not want to die
by my own hand like Plath, and when I sealed the letter
and sent it off, I hoped that if anyone could sense my
desperation it would have been my grandmother. I waited
for her help, and when a letter arrived without one word
that would tell me what to do I turned to my mother. She
had never been to Japan and, in an endless string of letters
I would never send, I tried to describe to her what had
become of my life.

I spoke to almost no one in Tokyo. I had no friends,
and when the opportunity presented itself for lunch or
dinner with a stranger, my Japanese was not good enough
to forge connections. I could ask, How are you? And
when the same question was asked in return, I could re-

spond, I am fine, I am okay. Once I learned the word for homesick. "Sabeshi," I responded with tears burning behind my eye sockets, but my dinner partner only nodded sympathetically from across the table, which had the messy effect of releasing the tears down my cheeks and into my lap.

It occurred to me that the Japanese I knew could talk endlessly about weather, but maybe it was only because of my language deficit that weather was always the big topic of conversation. I looked forward to the dramatic autumn storms when I could say with all the force of feeling how cold it was, how wet. I liked days when I could get what I wanted at the bank, the post office, the supermarket, without being asked to repeat myself because my accent sounded funny coming from someone who looked like she belonged but didn't. I reveled in the days and nights when, walking the streets of Shinjuku, Shibuya, Shimokitazawa, I'd be asked to join yet another strange man for coffee with the standard line, "Kohi e ikimasen ka?" I loved my nightly soaks at the public bathhouse where the scalding hot water would melt away my bitterness, and I both thrilled and reeled at having to strip off my clothes and bare my increasingly pregnant body to a roomful of women who witnessed my appearance and registered me at once as a stranger, an outsider.

Each night I bathed in a squat beside a dozen-or-so nameless women, all of us naked. Reflected in the waist-high mirror, my pregnancy should not have seemed any more anomalous to them than their clawed backs, exposed ribs, and shriveled breasts appeared to me. My belly was growing but the changes were still subtle. My waist curved gracefully, my hips had not flared, and my breasts were swollen in a way that was not unattractive. When I was able to ignore the roomful of eyes that made me so uncomfortable, I could feel how tender they were when I soaped them. My nipples ached less when I rolled them gently between my fingertips, and the water felt good when I poured it over my chest and between my legs, and even though I was convinced that the women at the bathhouse scorned me, I often took my time relaxing in the warmth and comfort of the steam. I told myself I was doing it for you. Besides, what did I care if my body was a source of gossip among strangers?

Then again, I wonder. Did they ever speak among themselves of my predicament? Could they, if they had to, pick my face out of a thousand others?

The fact is that I couldn't think of posing the questions that burdened me nightly to my mother because I was never able to tell her about you. My letters to her were as dry as "the golden autumn leaves in Yoyogi Koen" I bragged about; I hid you between lines about the "knick-knacks I bought to decorate my room"; I spoke with flourishes about "the nice man I had lunch with yesterday in Shinjuku." I dared not tell her how one of the few joys in my life that fall was the sound of maple leaves crackling between my fists and under my feet, or how I bought you a stuffed rabbit and then clutched it to my chest and cried all the way home on the train.

Testament to my secrets, her letters were equally cryptic:

Enclosed is a money order for the many expenses that must be adding up by now. I hope you are eating wisely and getting enough sleep. Love, M.

Then, it must have been November. It was dusk and I was undressing after an afternoon walk (to the yuhin-kyoku, a kissaten) when I heard my name being called from the outer hallway. "Hito-san? Hito-san, ir-rashaimasen ka?" It was a man's voice, and from the formal speech I knew it did not belong to anyone I knew. I padded down the hall in stocking feet and the messenger bowed to me. He wore a navy-colored uniform like a schoolboy and from his smile I could not detect that the news he carried was bad. I bowed back. Without a clue that my life could be worse than it already was, I returned to my room, tore open the envelope, and read the contents of the first telegram I'd ever received:

Nomi, Wnted u 2 knw Bachan died ths mrning. Cme home if u can. Let me knw. M

It makes me shudder to admit how selfishly I inter-
preted this news. My mother's mother had not lived in our
house the way Grandma Rio and Granny Reiko had, but
along with my mother and sister, I had visited Baachan
nearly every weekend of my childhood, had even decided
to study Japanese so I could speak with her since she
didn't speak English. I was close enough to Baachan to
have loved her, but it never occurred to me how grief-
stricken my mother had been at the loss of her mother,
that if I could not be sad for Baachan, I should at least
have been sad for her. Instead I received the news of
Baachan's death like an invitation. I'd been waiting for
permission to tell my mother about my pregnancy, and
what better way to make up for her loss than with the
news of a new life in the family.

Already it was late in the afternoon, but I threw on my
clothes, gathered all the yen notes I'd been saving, and
rushed to the telephone company to place the overseas
call to my mother. It cost over fifty dollars, which I paid
gladly for the opportunity to enter the soundproofed glass
booth with its connection home. I sat quietly for a minute
before keying in the number, catching my breath, letting
my confidence build, and it was in the silence before I
picked up the receiver that you kicked for the first time, a
feeling in the pit of my stomach like tumbling off the edge
of a cliff.

The ringing began: once, twice, three times, before

my mother answered. "Mom?" At the sound of her voice the tears began rolling down my cheeks. "It's Nomi."

"Nomi." Her voice was stern, unflinching. "Why did you take so long to call?"

"The telegram . . ." I stuttered. "It just came."

"It couldn't have just gotten to you. I sent it out last week."

"I'm sorry," I began.

"Why didn't you come home for the funeral?"

"I'm sorry," I said, but as quickly as the tears had begun to flow they dried. I could hear my voice going soft in my ears, my child's voice reserved especially for my mother, and specifically for all the times I'd failed her.

I didn't tell my mother that day, couldn't feel what would be my last opportunity slipping away. Life stopped after that; I don't know how I got home, or how long I sat staring in the mirror, out the window, into space, doing nothing. I slept, and the dreams I had then were dark and frightening.

I knew I could never return home. Within seconds my mother had made it clear that I was still her daughter, a child incapable of producing a baby myself.

You were lost to me, but I thought again to write to her. I sat down at my kotatsu table; I lay pen and paper neatly in front of me and the heater beneath warmed my legs while I slept. Once, thinking I would return to the phone company and try my mother again, I got dressed and walked as far as the train station before I realized it was too late. By that time, and way before then, it was already too late.

The loneliness I felt that winter was like nothing I'd experienced before. It seemed strange to me that I could be pregnant with a life that was part Porter's and have thought so little about him, but right then my life wasn't about him. Though I wrote to him daily, I never considered telling him about you. I said, *My Japanese grandmother just died in California, and I am here in Japan alone.* I said, *I miss you.* More than once, I even said, *I love you.* But I did not tell him about you. I carried you inside me, my biggest secret ever, and I did not say a thing.

I carried you in my body, but to all who inquired I lived alone those months in Tokyo. Separated from home by thousands of miles of water, I still belonged to my mother, and that knowledge was never far from my mind. If you were to become my legacy, you remained as silent as a stone entombed inside me, and me inside my room. And there, by myself, my mother waged a daily battle with me over your fate.

I wished to fill my days and nights with happy thoughts and pleasant images, but waking and dreaming I was not free. Having become heavy and lethargic in my sixth month of pregnancy, with no one to talk to and nothing but memory to fill my thoughts, I lived in my past, and your future was etched out of my memories.

When I was a child, my mother spoke to me in a language I did not understand. Only once did she ever tell me about her father. He went out to sea one morning and left his wife and children to starve. That was all she said, but it was a story that I committed to memory, and one that my mother herself believed.

My mother knew how to keep secrets. She guarded them like ancient treasure, a cache of ruby brooches buried away in her heart where even I could not find them. By the time I was born she had either forgotten about her secrets, or by that time they were down too deep to be retrieved. Often she'd begin to tell me things, then she'd stop. "We were very poor," she'd say. "We didn't have nice things like you and Melodie . . ."

I knew very little about my mother the night of her seventh wedding anniversary. She was preparing to go to dinner with my father while I stood transfixed in front of her dressing mirror, admiring her. She did not appear to notice me watching her, but I imagined words in the colorful language of lipstick, base, blush, powder, eye pencil, shadow, mascara. All the while my eyes never left my mother's beautiful face.

I wanted to ask if she'd miss me, the way I missed her when she was away, but already her thoughts were far away from me, fixed on some distant point in the mirror. I watched as she brushed powder over the silky smooth surface of her skin and penciled in her thin eyebrows until the radiant young woman in the mirror did not look like my mother at all.

"Tell me," I commanded when she bent down and allowed me to zip the back of her dress. "Tell me how you and Daddy met."

"At church," she said, slipping on shiny black pumps.

"Well, what else?" I did not want to be left.

"It was a long time ago." She examined her figure in the mirror, then turned and began walking away.

"Wait!" My thoughts turned inward from the image of my mother to the emptiness I felt at her imminent departure. "Did you always live in this house?"

"We came to live with Granny and Grandma when I was pregnant with Melodie."

"And before that?"

"Before that?" As if by magic, she sat down next to me on her bed and began smoothing her textured white bedspread. "Before that we lived in an apartment."

"Was it beautiful?"

"No," she chuckled. "Not at all."

"What?" I begged her not to stop. "What's so funny?"

"One night," she said, "I was in the kitchen fixing dinner and Daddy was in the living room reading—this was back when he was studying to become a minister. When he came into the kitchen for dinner his eyes were all red and shiny. 'I want you to fall back into my arms,' he told me. 'It's an exercise in trust.' And what could I say?"

"What did you do?"

"Trust means a lot to a marriage so I agreed."

"And what happened?"

"Well, I was quite a bit heavier back then."

"You were?" I found this bit of information impossible to believe.

"And he dropped me." She laughed.

I could think of no more questions. She was still laughing, but the story she told had terrified me. I slumped to the floor, scared for her, and suddenly I knew I couldn't allow her to leave me. She needed me to protect her, and sensing this I wrapped my arms tightly around her legs and inhaled her sweet smell down deep in my lungs.

I would not let her move, but could not keep her in one place either. Before leaving she kissed me once on the forehead and bade me good-bye. "Night night." She waved behind her. "Mind your Grandma Rio."

"And go right to sleep," she called from the doorway.

I would have followed her, but feeling too stunned and heavy to move I sat silently for the rest of the evening, and when the time came for me to go to bed, I tried to obey my mother's parting command as if obedience would keep her safe. I tried to sleep, but every time I closed my eyes I imagined my mother falling. She could have died. With my eyelids shut my mother fell again and again in the white headlights of each car that passed outside my bedroom window. Somewhere far away where I could not rescue her she was falling, and I listened to the rumbling of car engines, hoping at each fading that my mother would land. There was nothing to do but hope, until finally a pair of headlights steadied themselves on the ceiling above my bed, and the front door opened, then shut. My mother asked Grandma Rio about Melodie and me, and she said we were angels. "See there?" my father said, and I vowed to observe him very carefully after that.

My watching him was my own punishment for having failed to watch out for her. A small compensation, I knew, for my beautiful mother with no one there to catch her, forever falling through my father's arms, through time and space, and all I'd been able to do at four was to wrap my arms around her legs, brace her as best I could for a fall she'd long since taken.

The heart distends time; in the heart time is stretched, and then stopped; the heart edits time, but I did not understand at four what I would know for certain from my room in Tokyo. My heart placed my mother's once telling me that she had miscarried a child, her first, with the memory of falling. Awake and dreaming, I saw my mother falling again and again, but I could not make the connection between "falling" and "loss." I watched my mother fall, and I dreamed the same dream I'd had so many times before. I was doomed to fall through a darkened sky until I could taste my mother's loss in my own blood and what I had sensed for so long came true. One afternoon the dream ended with me crashing to earth. I landed face down, my face buried into my pillow, and every part of my body ached, but the only sign I needed was a cut in my lip where my teeth had bitten through, and I awakened knowing that my mother would never fall again. She had been pregnant the night my father had made her fall back into his arms, and with this knowledge I felt a void, and a sadness I had never known.

I missed my mother, and while I should have been preparing myself to be a mother, I wanted only to be her daughter again. Because of my mother's loss, I examined my own memories. I turned my mother's loss around in my mind like a treasure, considering always its impact on me. I wanted to ask what it had been like for her to lose her first child, and with him perhaps a part of herself, but I kept the questions I wanted to ask of her to myself and so kept my mother's memories alive for her in a way she could not do for herself. And in this way, the giving up and the leaving began long before you did, though it would all end with your birth.

When the time came, I knew where to go. I had a doctor, Hasegawa-sensee. He spoke English, knew enough to say, "Spread your legs." "Don't worry." "This will hurt, but don't move." He worked out of a hospital in Shibuya, not far from my four-and-a-half-mat room, and shortly before midnight, when the contractions were coming regularly and strong, I packed a suitcase and walked down to the street to hail a cab. I told the driver where to go—the name of a hospital I no longer recall—and he took me there. Maybe Hasegawa-sensee was called, maybe he wasn't, but he never showed up. Other doctors were there, or maybe they weren't doctors. Maybe they were interns, nurses, orderlies, I couldn't tell. The only thing I could be certain of was that no one at the hospital spoke English and my Japanese wasn't good enough. They talked to me kindly, reassuringly, but I will never know what they said. I could say, "Hasegawa-sensee wa doko desu ka?" Where is my doctor? But when they said *mada*—not yet—I could say no more.

I couldn't ask what was happening to me, when the pain would end. I could not keep track of time, though I know that labor lasted through the night. I know that I labored and cried and tried not to scream or fall asleep, and that once a clock read seven-thirteen and I didn't know whether it was morning or night.

But what I regret more than everything I could not have known was that I never held you. Long before you were due I told Hasegawa-sensee that I was to be given no medication during labor. I would give you up, but I did not want you to be taken from me. I wanted to know when you were being born; I wanted to hold you once, to give you away because then I could always know for sure that you had once been mine. He said that that was fine, that Japanese women were almost never medicated. "Don't worry."

When he did not come to the hospital I told everyone who would listen no medication. I tried not to show my pain, and when they tapped my spine and attempted to stick me with a needle, I fought them. I fought them with all the strength I had until I no longer knew why I was fighting, what cause, or whom, and then I found myself lying in a row of other women, in a room I had not seen before. It was morning then, gray and wet through a barred and filthy window. I stared at the day without the strength to do anything else until Hasegawa-sensee appeared at my side. I must have looked bewildered because he said, "You're finished now, Nomi, it's all over." Then he took his hand and very gently wiped a wet spot from my cheek.

I should have brushed it away. I know. I should have broken his arm. I should have sat up and yelled and demanded to know where they had taken you, but I didn't. I let Dr. Hasegawa touch my cheek, I absorbed his touch with my whole body, and I think I cried, very softly, that I could not remember.

"Amnesiac," was the word he used. I was given an amnesiac. Because he wasn't there, for one. Wasn't called in time, he claimed. But it was hospital policy for cases like mine, he said. For the sake of the woman it was better not to know.

I did not argue with him. I do not know why. But late in the afternoon when I was strong enough to walk out the door forever I passed the room where the newborns were kept. I stopped outside the glass and examined each face and I might have seen you there, though I can't be sure. All I really knew was this: I didn't give you away, never held you, couldn't understand then that I was giving up a part of myself I could never reclaim. I left Japan thinking I was leaving behind parts of my mother and grandmother that I didn't want, parts of myself that I no longer needed. I confused leaving with being left, and I must admit that my heart still does not understand the difference, except for this: You were mine alone until you breathed your first breath in this world, and after that you were gone.

1 0

·

N o m i

I left Tokyo in the early morning when the sky was just beginning to open its eye on the day. Until then, mine had been the world of the night. I had walked the streets of Shinjuku in darkness, when my pregnancy would seem least conspicuous, and I'd preferred it that way. I liked to watch the Japanese drag queens come out in their wigs, short skirts, and high-heeled shoes. I'd seen transvestites before, on Polk Street when I was a child, but in Shinjuku they seemed lonelier, their gait more desperate. Or maybe, trapped inside my pregnant body, I was the lonely one. I'd travel by train from Shinjuku to Harajuku or Roppongi where young Japanese women flaunted their dyed-red hair and matching lipstick. Then I'd board the last train with the drunken, blue-suited businessmen with their glazed eyes and together we'd stumble onto the platform and amble home. But I never stayed up long enough to notice the charade of life that took shape in those early hours of morning. Against a backdrop of glass and cement, old women carried wicker baskets on their heads like I imagined they did in Third World countries; shopkeepers lifted their steel doors and filled their bins with ice and fresh fish. I took my seat on the bus that would take me to Narita, to the plane that would take me back to the States, and I rested my head on the brocaded white seat back, clean and unstained. I listened to the woman at the front of the bus greet each new passenger with high-pitched politeness, and I watched the sun color the sky like the pink inside of a grapefruit knowing that my year in Japan had come to an end. I would make it back to school for the fall semester; I would return as if nothing had happened, my mind cleansed of memory, every trace of what had become of me the year before gone.

As the summer ended, my parents had written to me often, practically begging me to tell them I was coming home. I had thought to write back, but for a time I couldn't think about them. Staying or leaving were the same, until I finally made my decision to return, and then I told only Porter.

The ten-hour flight evaporated over the time line, and for reasons I could not comprehend, I arrived in San Francisco the same morning I'd left Tokyo. I didn't tell him why I'd left Japan so abruptly and, as if following some unspoken agreement, he didn't ask. Instead, he held his arms out to me, and I accepted his refusal to ask questions like the promise of a miracle.

For a time, only Porter was real. He had a past, which he told me about. Parents, sisters, brothers, a dog named Chelsea and another called Samson, a rabbit named Jake, and Jasper the cat, and they were all my family too.

I learned their names. I knew what each one looked like. Some were dead, the way I'd once suspected they were, others unreachable in a foreign city. Only at night, after a glass of wine, a bite to eat, a cigarette or two, did they come alive. His father was an ambassador, a doctor, a thief who stole the heart of his mother, a jazz singer, a whore, a madonna. I listened to his stories and they reassured me that nothing had ever happened in my life worth mentioning.

One night, when he asked about me I told him, "I am Nomi of the starched sheets. Nomi of the clean white walls."

"Can I write on you?" he asked.

"Uh-huh," I said, and he took his finger, an imaginary crayon, and colored me red, orange, yellow, green, blue, until I was laughing the laughter of fire and sun and sky. I closed my eyes and laughed so hard that they leaked water from the sides and he licked away the tears.

Only it wasn't like before. There was a stone inside me where you had been and no amount of my wishing would make it melt. He knew, of course, that my passion was feigned, knew about the stone and maybe even figured he could melt it. With all the force of a rushing current, he bore down on me, but the stone remained buried in a part of me that he could not touch. And because he hadn't known me long enough before I'd vanished, he mistrusted his memory instead of mistrusting me, or maybe he clung to it.

If he wanted to make love, he'd have to take me by surprise, trick, or cajole me.

"Time for a nap," he'd say, or he'd come up from behind when I was brushing my teeth or washing dishes, or wake me from a dead sleep.

Late in the afternoon, he slid the hair band off my head and, quickly undoing two buttons from my blouse, pulled it up over my head and unfastened my bra. Then (had I fallen asleep?) he slipped under the covers, unzipped my jeans, and began tugging at the waistband with his teeth.

"Careful," I said, as if his teeth were what frightened me. I awoke quickly, horrified that he would notice the stretch marks, touch the excess skin that still hung around my belly where you had been, and then he would know. Or maybe he already knew.

"Shhhhh," he whispered, his voice muffled under the covers.

He left my panties twisted around my ankles and moved on to other parts of my body. I kicked my feet trying to free myself, but he rolled me onto my stomach, and then I knew it was useless to fight. I could have been anyone then, with him riding me like a horse, me bucking from below. Thinking that the movement beneath him excited him, I stopped, lay still for as long as I could, but something inside me would not lie still for long. Soon I was moving again, fighting him fighting me, until the weight of his body fell heavy against my back and his breathing became even and slow against my neck and he slept. Porter, the gatekeeper, slept, and I slept too, believing in my release.

I got very good at sleeping. After Tokyo I could sleep through anything. Sleep took me away from Porter, my mother, my father, my grandmother, and sometimes in my dreams I found you. I didn't see you exactly, in my dreams I didn't know what you looked like, but you came to me in a fish dream. At first it was always the same. A single blue fish, swimming along the shallows of a perfectly clear pond. I saw it there and I watched it swim with a feeling of contentedness. There was never anyone but me in this dream—the fish and me, me watching the fish swim. Then the fish began to jump and I could see that it was not as big as it appeared in the water, though its scales were all silver and light. Each night it jumped closer and closer to me and the first time it landed in my arms I didn't quite know what to do with it. I stood there, unprepared; I woke up. Then one night I cut it open. I sliced it along the underside from the gills down the center to its tail as if to clean it, and I examined its entrails. Heart, liver, spleen—I touched the slippery organs with my fingers. They felt warm with life. The heart beat in my hand, the liver glistened the tangy brown of blood. And always when I woke up from this dream it was as if I had spent the night with you.

I told Porter. Whenever I dreamt of the fish, as a way of introducing him to you, I announced proudly that I'd had the fish dream. *Ah*, he grinned, *the fish dream*.

Sometimes he said he could tell by the way I smiled, contented in my sleep, that I was dreaming of the fish. When this happened I felt very, very happy, imagining that he knew of you and approved.

Then one night in November I came home from a late class and Porter was gone. No trace of him, no note. The way I rummaged through his closet it was as if I had been a detective my whole life. I checked the floor first, and noticed that the only items missing were his running shoes; above on hangers his shirts were all there, all hanging in a row smelling like the earth. When my search was complete I determined that he was wearing running shoes, khaki pants, a jeans jacket, and his brown leather coat.

That night, because he did not return by nine, not by ten or eleven, I lay awake. By midnight I was certain he was dead; by one in the morning I hated his guts.

It was three forty-six when he returned. Not wearing a

leather coat, jeans jacket, or running shoes, only the khaki pants like I'd imagined, and it occurred to me the instant I saw him that his running shoes sat propped up in the hallway, and that his leather coat had been at the cleaners for two weeks, and I made a mental note to retrieve it next time I was out. His eyelids were heavy and I couldn't tell whether he'd been drinking or crying. "Where have you been?" I demanded.

"I needed to think," he said, very quietly.

"I'm not asleep, so you don't have to whisper."

"I needed to think," he said, loudly now.

I almost laughed. For a minute I was so happy he'd come home, that he was not dead, that I forgot how angry I'd been. "Think about what?" I asked.

"I want us to have a history."

"What are you talking about? I thought you were dead."

The droopy lids half-masking his eyes were like heavy curtains parting on a tragedy I understood nothing about. In less than two minutes I'd gone from alarm to joy to anger and back to alarm. This was about Porter, about his disappearing, only now it didn't seem to be about him at all.

"Your mother called," he said at last.

"What?" I had imagined him dead, the way I'd imagined my mother when she left me at night as a child, but I did not understand why.

"Your mother, remember her?"

Maybe I had only wished her dead, wished Porter dead. "How did she know I was here?"

"Evidently it took quite a bit of searching."

"What did she say?"

"She wanted to know how you were."

"What did you tell her?"

"I told her you're fine. You are okay, aren't you?"

Probably he noticed my clenched jaw, and the way I couldn't stop shivering. Or maybe he knew about you. "Don't tease me. What else did she talk about? Tell me everything she said."

"Don't worry, your secrets are safe."

"What are you talking about?" I'd had enough of his taunting. I lunged at him, but he grabbed my arms and held me inches from his face.

"I'll tell you everything," he said. "Okay?" Slowly he released his grip and seated himself beside me on the bed.

"The phone was ringing when I walked in so I dropped my books at the door and picked it up and she said, 'Hello, is this Porter?' And I said, 'Yes.' And before I could ask who was calling she said, 'This is Tomoe Hito. I'm Nomi's mother, and I was wondering if I could speak with her.' "

"Oh my God."

"And I said no, you weren't home, and I told her I'd ask you to call her, but she didn't seem to want that."

"Oh my God."

"I think she wants to respect your privacy. The only

thing she seemed to want to know was that you were here and okay."

Porter became silent, but I could see his thoughts circling like the citrus trail of lemon in gin. "I'm sure you have your reasons for not telling her, and you're entitled to those, but you're lucky to have your family around, and you shouldn't just disappear on them, it's not right. Christ, I didn't even know what to say to her."

"I'm sorry."

"No, you're not."

"No, I am."

"You're not, but the thing is that you're safe now. Come here," he said.

And when I did, he cradled me in his arms and rocked me back and forth and stroked my hair. I could not cry, but I felt close to tears, and closer to him than I'd felt since I arrived back. "I don't care what happened to you in Japan," he whispered, almost cried. "I care that something happened to change you, but whatever that is is your business, okay? If you don't want to tell me, I won't ask, so you don't have to be so goddamned mysterious, okay?"

It would be morning in less than two hours, but once he was finally beside me in bed neither of us could sleep. He stroked my hair, his eyes wide open, and his fingers grazed a scar below my hairline. "When did you get this?" he said, suspiciously.

"It's nothing," I said.

"It wasn't there this morning."

"Yes, it was, and yesterday too. It's ancient."

"Then how did you get it?"

He was the one who'd been gone half the night, not me, but I sprang up ready to defend myself. "I was perched over the metal railing of a shopping cart, being pushed by my mother through the checkout line . . ."

"So you do have a mother."

"Very funny. 'What a beautiful boy,' the cashier called me, and she was right. About the way I looked, I mean. I have pictures of myself at that age. I had a rice bowl haircut clipped just above my eyebrows, which were bushy back then, and dark, curious boy eyes . . ."

He stroked my eyebrows. "What happened here?"

"I tweeze them."

"Let them grow."

"Okay. Let me finish."

"My mother wanted a boy when she was pregnant with me. A year before she had had my sister, Melodie . . ."

"You have a sister?"

"Let me finish. She had thought all along that I would be a boy. And then she was horrified when the checker mistook me for one.

"So she paid for the groceries and strolled me out into the parking lot. It was fall, I think. I remember the wind.

"Then she belted me into the back seat. She always

made me ride in the back. My legs barely reached over the edge of the seat, so there was plenty of room for the shopping bags, which were on the floor in front of me.

" 'Don't touch,' she told me. She was always saying that.

"So I am all alone in the back, inspecting an apple poking through the top of a plastic bag. A red one, you know how they have little specks. Those specks used to remind me of stars. But then I thought, what if those stars are really only dirt—my mother was always listing off all the places dirt hid. So I unlatch my seat belt and reach out in front of me. I am grabbing for the apple when my mother swerves the car to the side of the road and leaps out into traffic. 'Stay here,' she says. And I don't know what happened next. I must have hit my head, I don't know on what, because the next thing I know my mother is no longer in the car. When I look out the window I can't see her, and then all of a sudden she's back and I can't bring myself to cry or ask where she's been because I don't want her to be mad that I unlatched my seat belt.

"I was ashamed of the blood. It stained the car seat and floor mats, but my mother didn't say anything. She drove me straight to the emergency room and after my head had been stitched I figured she'd tell me where she'd gone, but she never did. For years it bothered me. Every time I looked at my forehead, I'd think about it. Then I realized it wasn't important what my mother saw. Maybe she even slammed on her brakes on purpose."

"Huh," Porter said when it was clear that the story was over, "maybe she was drunk."

"Are you crazy?" I said. "No one in my family drinks."

"Maybe they should start."

"You are crazy, aren't you."

"Well, my parents drank and they seemed to enjoy themselves very much—while they were alive, that is."

"How did they die?" I asked, and it occurred to me then how strange it was that I had never asked this question before, though maybe he had told me. Had I forgotten?

"They were alcoholics," he said very slowly, spacing each word.

"I'm sorry."

"Don't be. I didn't tell you so you could feel sorry. In fact, I had a little to drink myself tonight."

I had smelled alcohol on his breath when he came in, and maybe I should have thought it strange, but I didn't.

"Oh yah," he said, before we drifted off to sleep that early morning. "I forgot to tell you. Your mother asked if we'd come out for dinner tomorrow night. She said she's cooking for your grandmother's birthday, and I said we would."

"Watch it," I tell Porter on the fourth step up the landing. "That step is higher than the rest." It is a reflex, something

I say without looking back, to warn visitors. I've been back home less than a minute, but already I am feeling proprietary.

My father answers the door. "Nomi." He hugs me, and I imagine a bridge, severed in the middle and burning, or is it a house? My life is a burning house collapsing in on itself. There is too much weight.

"Welcome home!" My father interrupts this thought. "It's nice to see you, baby, and this must be Porter." A hand is extended and met and greetings are made.

My mother is in the kitchen fixing dinner. I know that she has seen me through the doorway, but she does not rush to greet me. I watch her expression as she frowns at a platter of raw fish she has been arranging, then wipes her fingers on a hand towel before lighting the short distance to the door where Porter and I stand waiting. She has placed calls to Berkeley and maybe as far as Tokyo, but now that I have come home to her—safe, healthy, alive, and not ready to leave yet—she takes her time.

"Does Porter like sushi?" she asks me back in the kitchen.

I pause before answering. "Yes." She is not acting strangely, I tell myself, she is not mad at me. She is genuinely afraid that Porter won't have a taste for raw fish. "He loves it."

"Well, then," her eyes grow hard and determined, "I don't think there's going to be enough."

The platter is massive. Arranged by my mother's expert hands, it holds more pieces of maguro, hamachi, ika, tako, and mirugai than my eye can count. "You must be kidding," I try to reassure her. "It's beautiful, and there's plenty."

"Do you think so? I'm afraid it won't be enough. I knew it wouldn't be enough, but when I went back to Henry's Fish Market it was closed. He closes early on Sundays, you know, so I went to Lucky's to see if I could find something to serve on the side, but I couldn't think of what else to make in so little time."

"Don't worry," I say. "There's plenty."

"Okay," she says. "Oh, I know. I could make some sunomono." Gliding away from the platter in one swift motion she throws open the refrigerator and, in a squat, begins rummaging through the vegetable bin. "Oh no," she says. "Just two cucumbers. That won't be enough."

"I'll go get some more," I tell her.

"No," she says, "you just got here. I'll go."

"Don't be silly," I argue. "You're busy here. Porter and I will run out."

"Well, okay, then," she says. "But don't be too long. I don't want the fish to spoil."

"We'll be right back."

Porter is standing in the living room, holding a wine-glass full of sake, talking to my father. I wait at his side for a minute, and then I take the glass from his hand and drag him away by the arm.

"Where are we going?"

"To the market."

"What's the hurry?" he asks when I sail through a stop sign and fly over the crest of a hill, bottoming out the car. "You could at least tell me where we're going, maybe even give me a little tour of Nob Hill if you're going to drag me out like this."

"Shut up," I tell him.

"Why are you being so nasty?"

"Because I'm in a hurry, that's all." I, myself, don't know why I am rushing. Is it to get away? To get back? "My mother needs cucumbers, and we've got to get to the market before it closes and if we're not back soon, then dinner will be late."

I can feel the tears welling, but I throw my head back and concentrate on the steering wheel clamped between my fists. "You shouldn't drink around my parents," I blurt out without knowing why.

"Okay," he says, "but what's the rush?"

When Porter and I get back with the cucumbers it is as if I were arriving home for the first time. Melodie is there with her new boyfriend Mark, Grandma Rio and Grandpa Tadashi have come up from downstairs, even Granny Reiko is at the table, and my mother has decided that there is enough food after all, without the cucumber salad.

"Nomi, come here," she calls to me from the table.

She seems to have forgotten that I've been here before, that unlike everyone else I haven't just arrived. "Nomi," she sings my name, waving her hands merrily as if to bridge the distance between us. With my mother, one trip to the supermarket can erase two years away.

"Nomi . . ." She takes my hand. "And Porter, it's so nice to meet you." Porter bends over and embraces her there, at the table, and I watch as her body stiffens. She is the commander here; she is in control, and sensing this he pulls back.

"Sit down, Porter," she says without missing a beat. "I want you to meet everyone. This is Nomi's grandmother Rio, and her husband Tadashi, and you've already met Nomi's father Goro. And this is my older daughter Melo-die and Mark Ishida, and over there is Nomi's great-grand-mother Reiko."

Porter smiles at everyone and when he nods at Granny Reiko she squints at him and signals him over by jerking her head back. "You"—she winks at him—"sit here with me."

"Me?" Porter is confused, but flattered. He scoots his chair over beside Granny.

I am about to follow him, but my mother pulls out the chair next to her and taps it for me to sit. I long for Porter, can't imagine how I will make it through dinner without him at my side, but there is nothing I can do. I remind myself that he is not gone; I can see him there, at the other end of the table. I wait for him to turn toward me and when he does I wave, but he does not see me, only stares right through me, lost in a stupor of sake and sushi. Across from me, Grandma Rio doesn't look good. I can tell it's hard for her to sit at the table with everyone and she probably wouldn't even be here except that it's her birthday and my mother has gone through the trouble of fixing dinner for her. But there's more. She sits with her shoulders slumped and her eyes scrunched up and turned in as if she is concentrating on something inside her head, and I know it is me she came upstairs to see. She watches me from the corner of her eye, waiting for a gesture from me. She refuses to come alive until I notice her, and I am not ready yet.

I left her long ago, when I moved to Japan and gave you up, and now I must face what a terrible thing I have done. I am the malicious puppeteer holding her slack at the end of my strings, but it isn't as if I wanted it that way. I didn't ask for this, I'm thinking to myself, when I realize that Melodie's boyfriend Mark is speaking to me. "Tell us about Tokyo," he says.

"Tokyo is fine," I say. I have thought many times of things I'd like to say about Japan, but the image floating through my head now is not from there. I see the fish treading its tail through the water, very slowly, near the bottom of the pond. It will die that way, alone, without any air. *Poor fish, swimming there all alone.* Lowering my head I notice that the sweater I am wearing smells stale, like the hull of a plane, the plane that swallowed me, and I was inside, like being inside a giant fish, inside and then spit out.

"That's okay." Melodie, directly across from me, turns to Mark apologetically, and then to me. "I mean, if you don't want to talk about Tokyo right now . . ."

"You're looking good." Grandpa Tadashi grins at me from across the table and suddenly I remember the backyard. He has fish, too, lots of them. Ladyfinger, the fish Grandpa thought was full of eggs until it turned out she was really a boy, full of fish food and disease when I found her one day floating sideways. And Piggie, the silver fish with the smoothest scales—he used to kiss my fingers when I held them over the side of the pond. It's been so long since I thought of his fish, thought of him at all. I smile back across the table. "How are the fish?" I ask.

"Oh, they're doing just fine. Healthy, and big. You probably won't even recognize them they've gotten so big."

"How big?" I ask.

"This big." He holds his hands out sideways, a foot, maybe two feet, apart.

"Nah." The fish in my head is dying, its gills barely moving, its belly rubbing the bottom of the pond. "Not that big. Can Porter and I see them?"

"Why sure."

"After dinner," my mother says.

"Mmm-hmmm," Grandma Rio joins the conversation, "that was a good bite of fish."

"Yes," Melodie says, "the sushi is delicious."

"Good," my mother says. "There's plenty here, so eat as much as you want."

After dinner when Grandpa Tadashi walks Porter and me out back to the pond—my stomach full of sushi, my head brimming with sake—I begin to feel cold. The air is still, I tell myself, not cold, but I am shivering all the way up and down my spine and I cannot stop.

There is no moon. Grandpa Tadashi has sealed parts of his garden under a fiberglass roof and the three of us walk single file past rows of white orchid, purple fuchsia, pink azalea. The delicate faces of flowers dot the jigsaw of branches and green leaves poke at me from every direction and as I walk I breathe in the childhood smell of damp and fertile soil. I am aware that it is not cold in this garden where there can be no draft—the night air is still, but the knowledge that I should feel warm does keep me from shaking. I clench my teeth and focus on Porter's back in front of me, and in the distance, growing closer, I can hear the gurgling noise of bubbles splashing off the water's surface. The path to the fishpond is lined with a row of footworn flat stones which we climb in silence. When the pond appears it is smaller than I remembered, but it is the same. There is the fountain made of rocks where water rises from the back then flows into the pond, and beside me the child's chair where Grandpa Tadashi used to sit. I recognize it now as the chair that once belonged in my room—its white vinyl seat speckled with a pattern of gold stars now almost invisible. I recognize it and I am thankful it has been moved out here because my legs will no longer hold my weight. It is all I can do to keep my eyelids open, my gaze focused in front of me. The fish are asleep. They glide near the bottom of the pond, a slow parade of colors blurred by the silvery smooth surface of the water. Porter stands with Grandpa Tadashi at a distance from me. They are talking not far from where I sit and I strain to hear what they are saying. Porter's voice is full of curiosity and wonder, and then Grandpa Tadashi speaks and his words are slow and the sound that comes from deep in his throat shakes loose something inside me. *It is the fish, coming up from my throat.* I can feel its tail first, beating inside my belly, then struggling to pass through my ribcage and for a minute I cannot breathe. Shaking itself loose it gushes up my throat and into my mouth and I can taste it there. I open my mouth because I want to spit it out, but the taste will not leave me. The fish is not you, I am not dreaming, the taste in my mouth is of fish. I want to get up, I call to Porter, *he is so close but he is gone,* but all I can make is a gurgling sound, *air trapped beneath the water's surface,* and with my eyes open a hand touches my back and I am a child again and I can feel the calluses and cracks in the rough, dry skin moving along my leg, beneath the hem of my dress, inside my panties, up and down my buttocks and back, and I know that it is Grandpa Tadashi's hand. Moving up and down and I arch my back but I do not try to get away. *He is so sad.* I do not see his face, I never see his face, but it is not hard to tell how sad he is. Grandma Rio is the only woman he has ever loved, and I love her too. I have missed her all day and his hands moving up and down my back and buttocks say that he has missed her too, and make us both feel that maybe she is not gone forever.

The raw, fleshy taste is still inside my mouth, but I do not feel pain. My mouth senses my pain, but I feel nothing. I am scared because I know that it is not right not to feel pain, *maybe even to have felt pleasure,* knowing that what has happened to me is wrong, but I am not sorry. Grandpa's hands are touching my back, but it is Grandma he touches, not me.

I was only seven then, I remind myself. I am twenty-two now. There are sixteen years separating then from now. I swallow hard to clear a passage from my mouth down into my lungs, but what feels wrong and all that seems important now is not that what happened isn't right, but that I have mistaken the fish for you. It wasn't you I was dreaming about at all. It was myself I was remembering.

Grandpa Tadashi is gone now. I hear his footsteps trailing away and Porter is standing in front of me. I am not cold anymore but he is shivering. "It's chilly out here," he remarks. "Come on, let's go inside."

"Okay," I say, but when nothing inside me will move I take his hands and let him pull me up, and before going back inside I hold him for a minute there, by the pond.

11
.

Nomi Reiko Rio Nomi

Late that night I lay wrapped in Porter's arms, and while
he dozed I could hear his breath becoming even and
heavy behind me, but I could not understand how it was
that he slept. I stared in front of me at the darkness lit
occasionally by headlights that crept up the blank wall
toward the ceiling, then disappeared beyond an invisible
line. The passing cars sounded like waves breaking on the
shore not so far away and I remembered standing in the
backyard with my first boyfriend Eric, watching the white
water tear the shore and listening to his promise of
oceanic life. I remembered him and wondered if he had
gone to Hawaii the way he had hoped to, and what kind
of fish he had found. I remembered and wished the waves
that broke in my ears now would calm me the way they
had that afternoon. I did not understand how life could

turn so suddenly and what, if anything, had really changed.

Behind me Porter lay touching my back, my legs, breathing the thickness of my hair, anesthetized in my bed, asleep. Earlier, I brought him into the room where I had slept as a child. He touched the things that had been mine—on my dresser the green silk scarf that shaded the bare light bulb beside my bed, the body-shaped mug with outstretched arms and two broken fingers, frames holding photos of me with my childhood friends. He fingered my things and I tried to imagine it was me he was touching so tenderly, not bits of skin I'd long since shed. I followed him with my eyes, knowing that from now on my things would have more importance to him than they would ever again to me. Just as Grandma's touch made my childhood her own, Grandpa's hands made me invisible, and the hands of the doctor made you disappear, my story had become Porter's story. *All that I have left now is what remains untouched, fields of air left behind by the sleight of hand of history that made my story invisible, slipped it like a coin into Grandma's purse.* Out into the world and back again I had lost parts of myself I could no longer reclaim, but in place of all I lost I had Porter. I could never tell him what had happened to me by Grandpa Tadashi's fishpond, that night or sixteen years ago, or why the passion I'd felt for him had died, but these secrets, as invisible as airfields—like a child breathing inside me—were what held me to him. He and I were bound by a great, breathable force, and more surely than I had loved anyone I belonged to him. That knowledge was what I clung to and counted on.

My secrets were part of me now, a knot implanted where you had once been, and maybe he knew this because after touching the things that had been mine he had the urge to make me his, there, on my bed, in the space he now owned. With my mother cleaning the last of the dinner dishes down the hall, with the bathroom on the other side of the wall and its flushing water toilet sounds, with footsteps above and below and the memory of the pond still so close with me, he climbed on top of me and I gripped the sheet with my fists and prayed my pain would end soon. I was tired, and I wanted to sleep and not to have to think what had become of my life.

"I want to go home," I whispered to him afterward. "I want to leave right now."

"Why?" He did not want to hear what I had to say. "Dinner was fine. No one hassled you, did they? Tell me if they did."

"No." His breath smelled of sake, and not unpleasantly. A tear leaked out of the corner of my eye, but the scarf over the light bulb darkened the room and Porter saw only green.

Eventually I slept and dreamed of two jet-black crows with shiny orange beaks. I followed them to the shore and Porter was there and I took his hand and together we ran toward the ocean where we leapt feet first into the deep water and I kept sinking and sinking until my toes landed in the silty dregs. It was like the bottom of an aquarium, only it was really the ocean floor, and Porter was gone and I worried that I'd sunk down too deep, I'd never be able to breathe under so much water, but my body began to rise, very slowly at first, and in my lungs the water became air and I swallowed it in gulps and I knew I was still down too deep. Then I saw that the water had changed from deep blue to aqua until it was clear enough so that I could see the sun and I followed the light to the surface until the sky touched my face.

It was dark in the room when I awoke, but Porter lay close beside me. Softly, I called his name for comfort, and he wrapped his thick arms around me bidding me with his warm body and heavy breath to sleep.

A door opens, then closes; a car starts, then rumbles down the hill. Porter's leaving and returning became a ritual. After the first night, I never asked where he went. Like most rituals, the act itself was more important than whatever it might have signified.

It was like my father deciding to leave the church and my having sex with Richard. I was doing one thing while my father was doing something else, and those two things became confused, and the confusion shaped what was to come. I was ashamed of one thing, and my father of another, and because of our shame we could not see each other's misery. It was the same thing with Porter. I thought he left because of me. Because of you he hated me, and because he could not say so he left.

He left me again and again, but I could not see that his leaving had little to do with me. He went to bars to drink, which had nothing to do with me, or he went on another dig, nothing to do with me. He'd call me from Greece, Italy, North Africa, but I could barely hear his voice. I told him, Give me a signal to let me know it's really you, but the sun interfered and he couldn't hear me.

I paid the phone bills that told me he was where he said he'd gone—expensive phone bills, but I paid them gladly and stacked them in my underwear drawer because I found them oddly reassuring. They were my treasures, like maps left in the car long after the journey just in case I needed to get back there again. At night I dreamed of skyscrapers made of glass and jade-blue beaches and red buses on densely trafficked streets, street corners on which he did not stand. Even in my dreams, I could not imagine his wandering among ruins, holding a foreign coin. I'd think him gone forever, but he always returned. With glazed eyes and a throbbing head, or dried mud caked to his shoes and months of grime on his clothes which smelled like the ancient soil he'd dug up. Sometimes he returned ashen, other times suntanned.

Once, after a long time away, he informed me he wanted me to go with him next time. I remember because he said he wanted to make a baby in the ruins with only God watching.

He kissed my forehead. "I want you and me to be a family. We should have a baby," he said, just like that. "I don't know why, but we should."

What I heard was that you were alive. He had found you and now it wasn't only you and me but him too. And what he said was all he had ever needed to say.

I never told him about my trip to the abortion clinic. Rows of women dressed in ghost-like green lined up to be scraped, vacuumed, and sent home to get on with their lives. I requested no anesthetic and they complied. A nurse stood beside me, held my hand, spoke of my bravery. "What are you?" she asked.

"I'm sorry?" I stared up at her, wanting to understand.

"Are you Chinese?"

"No, Japanese," I informed her, "American." A dull pain pierced something inside me and spread outward to my fingertips. I squeezed the nurse's hand. There was strength in those eyes which I wanted for myself but I knew she would never let it go. There was cramping and the buzz of the vacuum clearing me out. But there was more. Why did I long to tell the nurse that I was raised in California? How I grew up with four generations of my family, and I am the only one who's ever seen Japan.

"She's Japanese." The nurse, no longer listening to me, looked past the white sheet that covered my abdomen, beyond the spread of my legs. "Oriental women," she said to the doctor. "They're all the same. They take the pain so well."

Because she wasn't listening I did not tell her that pain is nothing if it isn't life-threatening. I am not brave. I am Japanese-American, meaning one foot in either door.

It took Grandma Rio's dying to bring me home again. Faithfully, then, I returned. Alone, without Porter, I pulled into the driveway, and beyond the front windshield of my car and the interior window that led into the kitchen, my parents waited. They stood perfectly erect and spaced slightly apart, planted at the kitchen table like two carefully potted trees. I sat for a minute wondering what held them there. I imagined roots and water and gallons of soil, but there was something else too—something invisible. Though my mother did not gesture to me, her eyes narrowed on a spot inside me, her gaze held me rigid. I had seen that look in her eyes before, feared it for years until the day I feared leaving it, and finally I had returned.

Grandma Rio was thin. Looking at her blue-black hair and breathing in her familiar coppery scent, I could only ponder how translucent her skin looked, how hard it was not to envision bones and blood and a heart pumping beneath her skin, and how seeing her like that scared me. I had once vowed to protect her, but now I knew for sure that I had been wrong and my failure stared at me through swollen eyes. Maybe it was failure, or maybe it was love. I couldn't tell.

Every once in a while her lips would move; she would press them together as if trying to rid her mouth of something bitter, but no words would come out and after a while she gave up looking at me. I didn't know if she even knew I was there, in the room with her. I needed to call her back to me, but I didn't know what to do. Looking at her shrunken body and pale white face it wasn't hard to see death, but I could not imagine her death, so instead I envisioned my own. Her face had always been a mirror; it was I who was dying. "You're not going to die," I whispered. *You can't die.*

Finally one afternoon the blankness faded and Grandma spoke. "It's been cold here," she sighed, as if catching her breath after a long silence. "How was the weather in Japan?"

She was Grandma again and in an instant, then, it was like it had always been. "It varied." I shrugged, not wanting to remember, not wanting to forget.

"I heard it gets very cold in winter." She furrowed her brows and with her eyelids pressed tightly shut looked all of a sudden very, very cold.

"Right now," I said, "it is very cold. The wind blows in

from the Sea of Japan and no matter how many layers of clothing you wear you're always freezing."

"I can't stand to be that cold."

"No, I can't stand it either."

"How long will it last?"

"The winter?" I asked.

She paused. "You heard, didn't you?"

"Heard what?"

"About me. You know, I haven't been doing too well."

"Yes. I'm sorry."

"I know," she said, and then she sent me out of her room.

Shutting the door behind me, I thought she had made me leave because she was angry with me. I sulked all that night, and then the next day it was the same. During that week, I recalled all the afternoon conversations, the letters I'd written her from school, the one I wrote from Japan telling her about you. Maybe she had been angry with me all along. Or maybe she was angry now because she lay sick and dying and I didn't have anything to say. Maybe she knew that when I looked at her I saw myself. I couldn't see her because I was too angry with her. I didn't want her to die, not with my secret, not at all. I was the one who was angry and maybe she sensed this.

The important thing though was that I left knowing it had been her all along: I had gone to Japan to get away from her, but then I had missed her and in her absence I had coached Porter to be her substitute. It was not too late for him and me. He and I could continue—me with his history and him with mine. I would take him on and he would take on you.

It would never happen though. Our dreams together were always of the past. A mother, father, baby for him. And you for me. Together we had no future, but that was okay. It was how we both wanted it.

When I was alone, I didn't know if I missed him or missed you. Absence is absence. Already I was mad at her for leaving me. I had been rehearsing Porter, but there would never be anyone like her in my life. The conversation didn't so much matter—what mattered was the history itself. Grandma Rio would always be familiar, never be gone. But even so, what would I ever know for sure except that she had loved me.

■ ■ ■

Tomoe tells everyone I've been causing problems since Rio got sick but that's not true. I am an easy person to blame, but the fact is that I am the way I have always been and her judgment of me is unfair and inaccurate, though not unexpected. Nomi comes home, which makes me think the end must be near for Rio, because Nomi only otherwise visits on Christmas and maybe her birthday to collect her presents—she is that selfish. She has been here a week, fluttering around like a moth beneath me, talking to her boyfriend at all hours of the night. She is the one who is causing problems. But I know she will leave today because up she comes, all the way up the stairs to see me. (Tomoe with her good manners would not let her leave without saying good-bye to me even though she has not stopped by before this afternoon to say hello.)

Nomi has not been up here in years. Most likely she has even forgotten what it looks like up here, what I look like. She is not used to the way sick people, old people, her family, act, and this is not right for a young woman. She only comes to see me (I am a museum piece, a relic) because Tomoe has asked her to and then she climbs the stairs sheepishly, almost soundlessly, and I close my eyes and pretend to be asleep; let her watch me for a while. Let her breathe in the smell of sickness and age and decay—it's good for her.

Through the corner of my eye I can see her stroking my departed husband's samisen—how shameless she is! She plucks the strings, and then she picks it up and places it in her lap. Does she think I cannot see? Does she not see that I am watching her now with both eyes? I watch as she runs her fingers up the neck until her shamelessness is too much, even for me, and thunder escapes from my throat.

"You surprised me," she gasps.

I do not answer, let her be scared.

"Do you know who I am?"

"Queen Elizabeth?"

Her thoughts flash like a natural disaster across the television screen of her face. She thinks I am deranged.

"Nomi Nomi Nomi," I mock, and she lets her shoulders down, relieved. "Where's that nice man you brought with you last time?"

"Porter?"

"That's his name, that's right."

"He isn't here because this is not a social visit. I'm here because Grandma is sick."

I close my eyes, signaling her to leave. In less than five minutes I've had enough of her.

"Your daughter, Rio." She calls me back, refusing to leave.

"My daughter, yes. She has a disease, a cancer, they say." I am surprised at how easily the word "cancer" flows from my throat. Rio has a cancer; Rio has a new hat; Rio Rio Rio.

"She's going to die, Granny," she mutters. Does she think I don't understand? Does she think it's possible for a person, a household no less, to give one person this much attention and I don't understand? "Don't worry about Rio," I snap because I cannot take it anymore. "She's been dying for years. They say it's near her heart now and when it travels there you don't have long. But she holds on, she'll be all right."

"What do you mean?"

"Don't you think I wait every day, hoping Tomoe will come to me with the news. But has it happened yet? Will it happen soon? Probably not. If she's dying, that's one thing, but this has been going on for years, which is why you should know it's all a lie. They want you to think she's dying because, look, you're here, aren't you? But now I will tell you the truth. I'm the one they're talking about. I'm not as young as I once was, and I deserve to have some peace, but they lie to me. They will probably kill me with their lies, but I'm not giving up so easily."

"You're not going to die, Granny," Nomi informs me, "you aren't even sick."

She does not know what she says. She looks at me wide-eyed and I stare back. Behind her, in the mirror, I can see her black hair and my own white teeth. Even in old age I have white teeth and it is plain to see that I am not unattractive. My nose is strong, yet delicate, and around the eyes Nomi may even look a little like me.

■ ■ ■

They are here and they are gone. Like ghosts of bees they cloud my head with their black eyes, fat bodies, hovering wings. Melodie reads to me about green meadows, grassy hills, and desire like honey. Her voice drips in through my ear and sticks to my insides—sweet honey, I am a flower. Tomoe holds the receiver close. The cord stretches like a stalk connecting petals to soil. It is pliant, will not snap. I pray that it will not be cut. It is my umbilical cord and she is my mother. Tomoe, my kind mother, holds my life like a flower in her hands. But Melodie is Tomoe's child, not me, and her voice sticks to my ear like the paste of death. The bees swarm. They smell the honey, or do they make it? Goro is my son but he does not come. He calls and his voice sounds muffled and far away but he fills my head with music. His words float inside me, orange fish in a lily pond, making me forget everything but his voice. *I am a pond, a river, an ocean.* Goro is my child, good boy, orange fish swimming inside me. Tomoe holds the line. She has him on her line and she wants to rip him from me. *Let go.* She tries to pull the line away, but I hang on to the music. Orange fish beating his tail inside me, will not let him go, not so easily; yank at the line to free him, will not let her rip him from me, but he is already gone. Tomoe speaks to me. I am her child again. "Stop that, Grandma."

"Mustn't."

"No."

But she is not my mother. I will not listen to her raving, the tugging, the pain in my womb, the blood drawn from the hole in my womb. I am leaking life through my womb but there is no blood to catch. My blood is dried up, no water to wet my body, no honey. My mother is a tunnel, a dark cave, a papery nest, the bees are one bee, one giant hornet that stings me but refuses to die. I refuse to die, not yet, but I have been stung and honey gushes from me. Honey and mud, from Tadashi's garden, he is here. The bees are gone. He stands beside my bed, soiled beneath me, and the stench. Tomoe, my good mother. She turns me over and I fight her, mortified. Soil soiling soiled, I cannot bear that it must come to this. Tomoe cleans my behind and speaks to me. "It's okay, Grandma," she says. Though I hear the horror in her voice she forgives me. "It's okay now."

Then Nomi calls and all of a sudden I understand what they are trying to say. There is no music, no poetry. She is silent. I can hear her breathe. As if she is sitting beside me we listen to each other breathe, and I remember other times like this one, only her breathing now is punctuated by prayer. Okay, okay. Okay, she chants, *you are dying.* Okay, I understand now. I don't want her to go, but I must. The sound of her breathing is heavy. Her weight. I wait for her to say she is coming. I will wait for her forever, but she says nothing. I must go and she says okay. Okay.

Voices. Hissing. Suction that pulls me down but refuses to suffocate me, not yet. Hush. Whispers and waves. I breathe in and after a long while I exhale. Finally they are gone. The phone by my bedside rings, Nomi calling me back, but it stops. Nomi, it's those things you can't say that trap you in time and now there is no more breath. No more air.

■   ■   ■

I think of you all the time because there is so much I don't understand. I want to know why when you were mine I believed you did not belong to me. I had wished for you. You were what I wanted most in the world, but when I lived with you every day in my body I believed you belonged to Grandma Rio, not to me. Your fate was decided by my mother, not by me. You belonged to my grandmother and to my mother because I belonged to them, because that is what I believed.

You were my secret and because I kept you from Porter I began to imagine that my life was his. My life was a burning house waiting to collapse on itself, but I did not want to see the destruction. I tried to forget. I cried too many tears, poured too much water, tried to extinguish the flames with my silence, but now when I am left to sift through the ruins, though I can see that death is every-where I cannot stop. The fire has gone out, but I will do anything to quench the flames. It did not have to be this way. I could have lifted you from the wreckage, held you in my arms, made you mine, but it is too late. The house has fallen; there is too much water. Maybe that is what bound me to Porter. We were both fighting to save the house—drenched, drowning, cold, and alone. Grandma Rio is dead now but I cannot stop trying to keep her alive. I see her in the wind, and in my dreams she comes to me laughing, speaking her approval. And though you no longer belong to me, I once held you in my body and you are somewhere, mine.

Still, it is my mother's voice that speaks the loudest; my mother's voice that says the only way to survive is to make sense and go on. I worked all day and when I got home there was a message from my mother on Porter's answering machine saying I must come home. My mother said the doctors said Grandma was going to die soon, but I did not call her. I called Porter in Italy because I was scared and I needed to ask him what I should say. When I spoke to him late that night he said I didn't need to say anything. I should call and I didn't need to say anything. So I called.

"Nomi," she said, she knew it was me. My mother said she held the receiver very close to Grandma's ear and that Grandma clamped her eyelids shut, the way she used to do when she liked what she was hearing, when she was straining to listen. Over the phone the hissing of the oxygen machine beside her bed made me dizzy. It sounded like running water and I closed my eyes and imagined we were on a raft: Grandma and me, floating together into death. I had no words but I could feel her beside me, comforting me, listening for the approach of what? She couldn't talk and all I could say was okay. Okay, I said to her silence.

Mother, here is what also happened: I grew up, went

to Japan, gave birth, loved a man, and returned home. Faithfully, I returned and in a dream the night she died, Grandma and I rode together on a raft. I talked and she listened. She talked and I listened but her words were muffled by the gurgling of water which flowed until the ground beneath me became solid, arced in the shape of a bridge. From above the water I could see her floating face up, eyes closed, mouth still moving, only I knew what she had been listening for. It was me. She needed me to rescue her and I called to her, but the water frothed and followed its course and it must have been three in the morning when I sat upright in bed and realized what I needed to do. I called the hospital to tell her I was on my way, but the woman at the switchboard said it was too late. She said the best she could do was to connect me to the nurses' station and the nurse rang Grandma's room, but she didn't answer.

It is too late, I know that now, but I have something I need to say to her. I want to see her one last time because I don't want her to die with my secret. She knows about you; she knows who I am and I can't understand me, can't have you without her help. I do not know enough yet. Not about her or myself or what I am going to do without her. She never responded to my letter—the one I wrote to her from Japan telling her about you, and I need to ask why. I needed her to tell me and I wanted to forgive her.

I needed her forgiveness.

About the Author

Julie Shigekuni, a fifth-generation Japanese-American, was raised in Los Angeles and educated at CUNY Hunter College and Sarah Lawrence College, where she received a Henfield Award. She currently lives in Santa Fe, New Mexico, and is professor of creative writing at the Institute of American Indian Arts.